Dennis R. Maynard

The Magnolia At Sunrise

BOOK SIX IN THE MAGNOLIA SERIES

EPISKOPOLS.COM

WWW.EPISKOPOLS.COM
Books for Clergy and the People They Serve

ISBN: 1-4538-3425-7
ISBN-13: 9781453834251

COVER DESIGN

I am grateful to Chris Koonce of Fort Worth, Texas for designing the cover to this book. He is a very talented young artist. Chris earned a Bachelor of Fines Arts degree in 1991 from the University of North Texas. I encourage you to visit his website to view his portfolio of artwork. There are several opportunities for personalized gifts for yourself and others. He can also be a resource for fundraising opportunities for your organization, parish or school. Please visit his website at:

www.kcfunart.com
ALSO
ON YOU TUBE AT KCFUNART

BOOKS BY

DENNIS R. MAYNARD

THOSE EPISKOPOLS

This is a popular resource for clergy to use in their new member ministries. It seeks to answer the questions most often asked about the Episcopal Church. Questions like: "Can You Get Saved in the Episcopal Church?" "Why Do Episcopalians Reject Biblical Fundamentalism?" "Does God Like All That Ritual?" "Are There Any Episcopalians in Heaven?" And others.

FORGIVEN, HEALED AND RESTORED

This book is devoted to making a distinction between forgiving those who have injured us and making the decision to reconcile with them or restore them to their former place in our lives.

THE MONEY BOOK

The primary goal of this book is to present some practical teachings on money and Christian Stewardship. It also encourages the reader not to confuse their self-worth with their net worth.

FORGIVE AND GET YOUR LIFE BACK

This book teaches the forgiveness process to the reader. It's a popular resource for clergy and counselors to use to do forgiveness training. In this book, a clear distinction is made between forgiving, reconciling, and restoring the penitent person to their former position in our lives.

WHEN SHEEP ATTACK

Your rector is bullied, emotionally abused and then his ministry is ended. Your parish is left divided. Formerly faithful members no longer attend. Based on the case studies of twenty-five clergy who had just such an experience. What could have been done? What can you do to keep it from happening to you and your parish? Discussion questions included that make it suitable for study groups.

THE MAGNOLIA SERIES

BEHIND THE MAGNOLIA TREE (BOOK ONE)

Meet The Reverend Steele Austin. He is a young Episcopal priest who receives an unlikely call to one of the most prestigious congregations in the Southern United States. Soon his idealism conflicts with the secrets of sex, greed, and power at historic First Church. His effort to minister to those living with AIDS and HIV brings him face to face with members of the Klu Klux Klan. Then one of the leading members seeks his assistance in coming to terms with the double life he's been living. The ongoing ministry of conflict with the bigotry and prejudice that are in the historic fabric of the community turn this book into a real page-turner.

WHEN THE MAGNOLIA BLOOMS (BOOK TWO)

In this the second book in the Magnolia Series, Steele Austin finds himself in the middle of a murder investigation. In the process the infidelity of one of his closest priest friends is uncovered. When he brings an African American priest on the staff, those antagonistic to his ministry find even more creative methods to rid themselves of the young idealist. Then a most interesting turn of events changes the African priest's standing in the parish. A young associate undermines the rector by preaching a gospel of hate, alienating most of the women in the congregation and all the gay and lesbian members. The book closes with a cliffhanger that will leave the reader wanting another visit to Falls City, Georgia.

PRUNING THE MAGNOLIA (BOOK THREE)
Steele Austin's vulnerability increases even further when he uncovers a scandal that will shake First Church to its very foundation. In order to expose the criminal, he must first prove his own innocence. This will require him to challenge his very own bishop. The sexual sins of the wives of one of the parish leaders present a most unlikely pastoral opportunity for the rector. In the face of the ongoing attacks of his antagonists, Steele Austin is given the opportunity to leave First Church for a thriving parish in Texas.

THE PINK MAGNOLIA (BOOK FOUR)
The Rector's efforts to meet the needs of gay teenagers that have been rejected by their own families cast a dark cloud over First Church. A pastoral crisis with a former antagonist transforms their relationship into one of friendship. The Vestry agrees to allow the Rector to sell the church owned house and purchase his own, but not all in the congregation approve. The reader is given yet another view of church politics. The book ends with the most suspense filled cliffhanger yet.

THE SWEET SMELL OF MAGNOLIA (BOOK FIVE)
The fifth book in the Magnolia Series follows the Rector's struggle with trust and betrayal in his own marriage. His suspicions about his wife take a heavy toll on his health and his ministry. He brings a woman priest on the staff in face of the congregation's objections to doing so. Some reject her ministry totally. Then the internal politics of the Church are exposed even further with the election of a Bishop. Those with their own agenda manipulate the election itself. Just when you think the tactics of those opposed to the ministry of Steele Austin can't go any lower, they do.

All of Doctor Maynard's books can be viewed and ordered
on his website
WWW.EPISKOPOLS.COM
BOOKS FOR CLERGY AND THE PEOPLE THEY SERVE

FORWARD

Each morning the eastern rising sun illuminates the mountains that surround the valley I call home. At dawn the mountains first appear as shadowy figures against a gray sky. As the sun continues to rise, the sky becomes blue and the mountains actually appear to be pink. Throughout the rest of the day and into evening, the light and shadows continually dance off the mountains. They appear to be constantly changing. After the sun drops behind the mountains in the west, the light show ends. The mountains disappear into the dark sky. When the earth completes another rotation yet another light and shadow show is repeated.

My breakfast window looks out on one of the tallest of the valley's mountains. Naturalist John Muir described the view from the top of that mountain *as the most sublime spectacle to be found anywhere on this earth.* The winter snows crown this peak with a glowing crown of white each November. If we valley residents are fortunate, that snow remains until early June. The white crested San Jacinto provides us with postcard views for most of our season.

The Soboba Indians believe that there is a devil that lives at Tahquitz Peak on Mount San Jacinto. The legend is that they once had a chief that was much loved. Chief Tahquitz fell under the influence of some evil spirits and was transformed into a hated chief. When he died the tribe destroyed his body. His spirit escaped and resides on the peak. They point to the thunderstorms in the area as evidence of his presence. The legend is that a rattlesnake and a condor accompany his spirit.

For those of us that find our eyes continually drawn to the beauty of the mountain, it's difficult to conceive that any evil could reside in such a majestic place. For those of us that love the Church of Jesus Christ, the same can be said. Like the Psalmist, we are fed by giving thanks to God in the great congregation. We are nurtured when we praise the Almighty with other worshippers. The Great Eucharist lifts our souls. It inspires us to pour our resources into ministries to the poor, the sick, and dying. It is perplexing to come to terms with the reality that some in the great congregation, like Chief Tahquitz, have come under the influence of evil spirits.

The novels in this series attempt to take you inside the thoughts of those that see themselves as good while doing evil. I have tried to offer you insights into the persona of those that live daily with their own demons. The DSM or Diagnostic and Statistical Manual of Mental Disorders places labels on some of those that wreak havoc in the Church. When ministries, lives, and entire parishes have been damaged at their hands, a diagnostic label is of little comfort.

The behavior of some of the characters that reside in Falls City, Georgia cannot be found in the DSM. Their behavior finds its origin not in genetics or personality disorders. Disease in the soul is more revealing. Failure to do our own spiritual self-examination allows us to place ourselves on the throne of spiritual narcissism. From that throne we can pass judgment on others while granting ourselves a celestial pardon. The lives of the saints that we most revere expose souls convicted of their own unworthiness. Their ongoing repentance filled their hearts with compassion for others. Those most aware of their own need of forgiveness possess the most forgiving hearts.

Artist Chris Koonce of Fort Worth, Texas designed the cover of this book. Once again he has demonstrated his creative gift. I would like to encourage you to visit his website at kcfunart.com. You can also see his work on You Tube by entering KCFunart. This talented young artist offers a variety of products perfect for gift giving. They can also be used as fundraisers for your parish, school and organization. I am confident that if you give him a closer look you'll share my appreciation for his work.

I pray that your sixth visit to Historic First Church in Falls City, Georgia will continue to entertain you. I thank you for your devotion to these characters. I am grateful to all who continually encourage me to continue to let the story unfold. You are my best advertising. Without you, life in Falls City would have ended after Book One. Thanks for continuing to introduce your friends and family to Historic First Church. The ongoing drama of First Church has readers in every state in the union, Puerto Rico, The Virgin Islands, Canada and England. The list of folks that want to continue to visit Falls City continues to grow. This is due in no small part to you. For this, my cup overflows.

Once again, welcome to Historic First Church. I am so glad that you are here.

Dennis Maynard
Rancho Mirage, California
The Feast of All Saints, 2010

"We can only appreciate the miracle of a sunrise if we have waited in the darkness."
Author Unknown

chapter 1

THE REVEREND STEELE Austin was late! He had slept through the early service at First Church. He was driving as fast as he could to get to the family service. He glanced at his reflection in the rearview mirror. He hadn't even taken the time to shave. His dark whiskers protruded from his neck, chin and cheeks. His beard had never been so heavy. It looked like he hadn't shaved in days. He ran his fingers through his hair. The hair on the back of his head refused to lie down. He must have slept wrong on his pillow and now his hair would not cooperate. He had a cowlick. The only remedy for that condition was a shampoo. He didn't have time for that before he left home.

A stop light just one block from the parish property held him. He looked to the left and to the right. There were no cars in sight. Dare he run the light? He decided against it. The red light continued to stare at him. He thumped his hands on the steering wheel and shouted, "Come on, change! Change!" After what seemed like an eternity the light changed and his car bolted forward.

He whipped into the staff parking lot. "Oh, no!" Someone had parked in the space reserved for the rector. Every space in the staff lot was taken. He started up and down the rows in the parish parking lot. Every space was taken. He drove to the upper lot. None were available there either. He would have to park on the street. "This can't be happening," he pleaded. He drove around the block. All the parking spaces on the street were taken. Then he spotted a space two full blocks from the church, but it required him to parallel park. He wasn't sure his car would fit. It would be tight but he was desperate. He needed to at least give it a try. Slowly, carefully, he maneuvered his car into the space. He quickly exited his car and slammed the door shut. He started sprinting toward the parish campus. His legs were moving in slow motion. He was winded. His side hurt. His dress shoes cramped his feet as they pounded the pavement.

As he ran through the cemetery to the door outside the priest's sacristy he heard the organ music. The congregation was singing the opening hymn. He needed to get his vestments on and be seated in the pulpit chair in time for the reading of the Gospel. He was scheduled to preach.

Steele pulled his cassock from the clergy closet and started buttoning the several buttons. He had closed the first half dozen buttons when he realized he'd skipped the first one. He had to unbutton them all and start over. "This is unbelievable," he whispered in exasperation.

The door between the sacristy and the choir squeaked loudly when he opened it. A reader was reciting the first lesson from the scriptures. As he entered, every eye in the choir and congregation turned toward him. He felt himself blush with embarrassment. The congregation was packed with disapproving eyes. He attempted a smile but no smiles were returned.

The sextons had failed to place the pulpit chair in the sanctuary after last night's wedding. Steele looked around for a vacant seat. There were none. He had no choice but to go to the foot of the pulpit and stand there until time for his sermon. He leaned against the wall. The disapproving looks from the choir and congregation burned through his body. He thought the first lesson would never end. Then came the Psalm, the second lesson and a gradual hymn before the reading of the Gospel. Steele felt so conspicuous standing in front of the seated congregation.

At long last the Gospel Procession proceeded out of the sanctuary to the midst of the congregation for the reading of the Gospel. As they returned to the sanctuary Steele climbed the pulpit steps. He reached into his cassock pocket for his sermon notes. The pocket was empty! His shaking hands searched the other pocket. He unbuttoned the top buttons on his cassock and searched the inside pockets. A cold sweat broke out on his face as a slow panic rose up in him. He wiped his face with his sleeve. The congregation was staring at him. Nausea washed over him. His entire body was now trembling. He remembered he'd left his sermon notes on his study desk at home. Desperately he searched his memory for a glimpse of what he'd prepared. His mind was blank. He couldn't even remember the first sentence, let alone the point of his sermon. He was in a state of panic. The music had stopped. Everyone was staring at him. The silence was so awkward. He motioned for the congregation to be seated.

He forced himself to smile once again. "I fear that I've done a foolish thing." He chuckled but the gathered flock did not echo his chuckle. The congregation just glared at him.

"I know that you are aware that I overslept this morning. I fear I can't hide that from you so I beg your forgiveness." Again, he smiled at the worshippers but none returned the favor.

Steele felt the contents of last night's dinner pushing against his throat. His entire body was now drenched with sweat. He was so ill he just wanted to go lie down. His voice shook as he continued. "I want to assure you that I did prepare a sermon for you this morning, but I left my notes on my desk at home."

Some in the congregation began shaking their heads in disgust. He heard Ned Boone say in a voice that echoed through the church, "I tried to tell all of you that this guy is a loser." Several in the congregation nodded and muttered their agreement.

"Please, I think that I can give you a brief summary of what I've prepared." Again, Steele forced a smile as he felt the sweat run down his face, arms and legs. But not one word formed in his throat. He couldn't remember a single word he'd written. He opened his mouth to speak but there was nothing there but the vile taste of undigested food. Steele felt himself grow dizzy. His knees grew weak.

Elmer Idle stood and faced the congregation. Elmer shouted, "We tried to tell all of you. We agree with Ned. This guy is not fit for the First Church pulpit. Come on Judith, we're leaving."

At that Ned, Elmer and Judith exited their pews and started down the aisle to the back of the church. To Steele's shock others in the congregation followed them. Steele began pleading with the people to stay. "Please don't leave! Please don't leave! I'll think of something to say. Please.... Please.... Please..." Then Steele felt a hand on his shoulder. Someone was shaking him.

"Steele...Steele...honey...wake up...wake up."

Steele opened his eyes to see a worried look on Randi's face. Steele, you were having that nightmare again.

Steele nodded. He was so weak. His entire body was bathed in sweat and he was shaking. He was so cold that even his teeth were chattering. Randi got up and took the blanket from the quilt holder at the foot of the bed and covered him with it. "Honey, you are wringing wet. As soon as you quit shivering, you need to get up, take a shower and put on some clean pajamas. I need to change all the bedding. It's soaked."

Steele continued to shake under the blanket. His body was drained of all strength. "Did I scream?" His voice was more suited to a man three times his age.

Randi wiped the wet hair from his forehead. "Yes, you were screaming. That's what woke me up."

He closed his eyes. The shaking in his body began to abate. He tried to sit up but couldn't. "I think I just need to lie here for a few minutes. Will you stay with me?"

Randi reached under the quilt and took his hand in hers. "I'm not going anywhere. But Steele, you've got to get some help."

Steele nodded, "I know. I will." He stared into her beautiful face so filled with love and concern. "Randi..."

"Yes."

Steele grinned and in a voice that mimicked that of a two year old he asked, "Will you get me a drink of water?"

Randi smiled and squeezed his hand. "Welcome back, but don't forget what you promised. You're going to find someone to talk to."

Steele sat up in the bed. "Okay, but first I'd like that drink of water."

chapter 2

MRS. ALMEDA ALEXANDER Drummond had devoted a considerable amount of time to the attire she would wear on this particular Sunday. In addition to being the most prominent member of historic First Church, she was now the wife of the acting rector. She shook her head and muttered, "No, I am not the wife of the acting rector. I am the wife of the rector. I told Horace this morning at breakfast that I wanted him to stop referring to himself as the acting rector. Steele Austin is on sabbatical for the next six months. During that time you, Horace, are the rector!"

Almeda studied her reflection in the large mirror sitting on the floor of her dressing room closet. She had made multiple trips to Atlanta to select a wardrobe that would compliment her new station in life. She had shopped first at Rich's in Lenox Square Mall. That had been her standby for years. But now her new station required more. So she went across the street to Phipps Plaza to see if Nordstrom or Saks could meet her needs. She let out a great sigh. Both of them had failed her so she returned to Lenox Square. Neiman Marcus proved to have the designer fashions that satisfied her.

She studied the bright chartreuse dress that draped her body. She was pleased that she'd been able to maintain her feminine figure. She turned so that she could see the back of the dress. She smiled as her eyes dropped to the shapely calves on her legs. She'd been careful all these years to watch her diet and to spend time in her home exercise room with a personal trainer. From the passion she was able to stir in Horace she knew that he still found her desirable. "Not bad for a woman of seasoned years," she smiled.

Chartreuse was not a color she would normally wear. In fact, when she'd seen it on others she considered it to be vulgar. But now, on this first Sunday, she needed to be seen. It was even more important to her that the congregation remembered seeing her. She was not taking her new position in the parish lightly. She had been making a list of several things that needed her attention. She had attempted to discuss them with Horace but he suggested she reconsider each of them.

"Almeda, I love you with all my heart and I think I understand you better than you understand yourself." His deep baritone voice always had the most soothing affect on her even when he was disagreeing with her. "I am only the acting rector. My job is just to hold the parish together until Steele returns. I don't want to rock the boat."

"No, Horace. You are not the acting rector. For the next six months you are the rector. I do wish you'd remove that word from your vocabulary. I've known Steele Austin longer than you have and I just know that he'll appreciate the few little changes I want to make during the time that you're the rector."

Almeda reached into the hatbox sitting on the seventeenth century chair adjacent to the mirror in her dressing closet. She was so proud of the chair. The black work embroidery was so well preserved on the seat. She took great care to insure that no one ever sat on it but her. It also proved a good resting place for her hatbox. She removed the hat from the box and placed it on her head. It framed her face ever so nicely. She pulled at the slight veil on the front of the hat so that it shaded her eyes. She wanted to be able to observe the congregation without them being aware that she was doing so.

"Horace, you know that I always wear a hat to church."

"Yes, honey, and you always look so beautiful in them."

"Then you wouldn't mind if I gave Steele's secretary instructions to add a note in the worship leaflet? It would instruct women and girls to cover their heads in the church."

"Almeda, I know you mean well, but women stopped covering their heads in church in the 1950's."

"Not all women. I still believe that I should do as the Bible instructs. Don't you think we should follow the teachings of scripture?"

"Honey, of course I do, but we don't follow every instruction. The instructions have to be considered in the context of the time and circumstances they were written."

"Horace, it's such a simple thing. We could place a basket of head coverings at each of the doors for women who forget to wear a hat."

"Almeda, the women in today's world just aren't going to return to that practice, not even in Falls City. You are just setting yourself up for a major disappointment."

Almeda grimaced. She didn't like having anyone reject her ideas. She particularly didn't like having her husband do so. She decided to try a new strategy.

"I think I will at least discuss it with the altar guild. Perhaps we could all set the example."

Almeda arrived at the church a full thirty minutes before the service was to begin. She had instructed the sextons to arrange all the hymnals and prayer books in the pews to be facing outward and turned in the same direction. She wanted to make sure they had followed her instructions. She then inspected the flower arrangement. The vase on the right appeared to be slightly off balance, so she removed a couple of the flowers so that the two vases mirrored one another.

"Mary Alice!" Almeda called for Mrs. Gordon Smythe, the chair of the altar guild.

"Yes, Almeda." Mary Alice answered as she came out of the sacristy adjacent to the altar sanctuary.

"Do you see this candle?" Almeda pointed to the candle standing on the right side of the altar.

Mary Alice reached for the reading glasses hanging on the pearl chain around her neck and put them on her face. She studied the candlestick. "What's the problem?"

"Mary Alice, do you need a new prescription? Look, there's a fingerprint right there on the base. And look at the candle. The wick has not been trimmed to the same length as the one on the other side."

Mrs. Smythe studied the candle and candlestick more closely. "Well, I don't think anyone would see that."

Almeda put her hands on her hips. "I saw it, Mary Alice. I am putting you and the entire altar guild on notice that while my husband is rector I will not tolerate any sloppiness. Now before the congregation gathers, I want that candlestick repolished and the wick trimmed. I am instructing you to send a postcard to all the members reminding them to wear gloves when handling the candlesticks. Tell them to make sure the candle wicks are trimmed to equal lengths after each service." Almeda then turned on her heel and proceeded to the narthex to inspect the Sunday worship leaflets. She'd left instructions with the church staff that no misprinted bulletins were to be left for the congregation.

After she had completed her checklist of inspections, Almeda seated herself in the first pew of the south transept immediately under the pulpit. For decades her seat had always been third pew right hand side in the nave. She now needed to position herself so that she could better inspect the processional ministers, choir, and the congregation as they approached the communion rail. The service had not even started when she realized that she'd made the correct decision.

She could hardly believe her eyes. In fact, she had to lift the veil on her hat to make sure she was not seeing things. But there immediately across from her was a woman entering the north transept wearing a pantsuit! Almeda drew herself up in the pew as her entire body tensed with anger. "Now that is something that I simply will not tolerate." She shot the woman a harsh look. The woman attempted a smile but Almeda glared at her. The woman blushed and sank into her pew.

The anger continued to rise up in Almeda. She resolved to not even address this issue with Horace. She'd handle it herself. She would see that the proper announcement would be placed in next Sunday's worship leaflet. No, that would not be enough. The notice would have to be placed in the parish newsletter as well. She began to formulate the notice in her mind. *"Out of respect for Almighty God all women regardless of age are to wear dresses that come at least two inches below the knees in this House of Worship. Pantsuits, jeans or pants in any form more suited for field work are not appropriate."*

Almeda smiled and then expanded the note in her mind. *"Gentlemen and young men over the age of two are expected to wear ties and jackets."*

chapter 3

SEAN EVANS SIMPLY could not stop smiling. His only moment of sadness was when he realized that his mother would not be at the service ordaining him a bishop. But then, he did believe in the communion of the saints. He was comforted by the thought that his mother would be with him in praise and prayer. He had spent the morning of the election on his knees. He had set up a prayer desk in his living room. He put a crucifix on the wall. Incense was placed in the burner and he had lit candles throughout the room. He was determined to remain in prayer from the time the electing convention was convened until the results were announced.

His friend Jim Vernon was canon to the outgoing Bishop of Savannah, Rufus Peterson. All the candidates had been assigned a contact person. His contact person was Jim. They were told that their contact would telephone them after each ballot and inform them of the results of that ballot. It was believed that if any candidate was receiving only a handful of votes, they could then withdraw from the process and thus save themselves unnecessary embarrassment. It was further considered that if the election had come to a stalemate, one or the other of the candidates could withdraw, thus allowing the convention to elect a bishop without undue stress.

Jim telephoned Sean before the first ballot was even taken. He advised him that the bishop had ruled that the results of each ballot would not be announced. None of the candidates would be telephoned until a new bishop had been elected. He then whispered into the telephone. "But I'll be calling you after each ballot. Just don't let anyone know."

Sean started to object but Jim hung up the telephone. At precisely 9:00 a.m. the convention was convened. Sean Evans dropped to his knees at his prayer desk. He was determined to remain there. He rose only to answer the telephone, put more incense on the burner, or go to the bathroom. He held his rosary in his hands and recited the mysteries over and over again.

His bishop and clergy friends had offered to come to his condominium and spend the time watching with him. He had declined their offers. "I really want to be in prayer as Jesus prayed. Our Lord faced the great moments in his life praying in isolation. I want to do the same." He promised that as soon as he knew the results of the election he would call the diocesan office where he served as the bishop's canon and let them know.

His lower back ached and his thighs had long since lost their strength. He was sitting back on his heels with his knees still firmly planted on the prayer desk when the telephone rang after the seventh ballot. Jim Vernon was ecstatic. "Sean, you've been elected! Brother, you are now the Bishop of Savannah!"

Sean sat down in the chair at his desk. A joyful enthusiasm rose up in his stomach and spread through his entire body. "Are you sure?"

"This is the call, Sean. Or should I say, Bishop Evans. This is the official call informing you that you've been elected. Congratulations! We've done it. We got you elected. Now we are going to run this diocese like it's never been run."

"Wow! I hoped I would be elected but I guess I'm still filled with disbelief. I don't know, maybe I'm in shock."

Jim Vernon cupped the receiver with his hand so he could whisper into it without anyone hearing. "Sean, I love you. As soon as I can get to you, I plan to show you just how much. Tonight we're going to celebrate, just the two of us."

Sean whispered. "Thanks, Jim. I love you too. I'll look forward to seeing you."

Sean had no more than hung up the telephone until it rang again. This time it was the President of the Standing Committee of the Diocese. He informed Sean that the Standing Committee had just met and ratified his election. Sean thanked him and asked him to thank all the members of the Standing Committee for their confidence in him.

The telephone rang again within minutes. The Secretary of the Convention was calling to officially inform him that he'd been elected as the Bishop of the Diocese of Savannah and that he was in the process of filing all the appropriate papers with the various authorities. Sean thanked the Secretary and asked him to relay his gratitude to the convention delegates.

He had just placed the telephone back on the hook when it rang again. This time it was the Chancellor of the Diocese. "Canon Evans, you have been informed of your election as the Bishop of Savannah. The Standing Committee has confirmed your election and the Secretary of the Convention is filing all the appropriate papers. In my official capacity, it is now my responsibility to ask if you accept the election. Canon Evans, do you accept your election as the Bishop of the Episcopal Diocese of Savannah in the United States of America?"

A broad smile crossed Sean's face. "Yes sir, I humbly and prayerfully accept this election and beg your prayers, the prayers of the delegates and the prayers of all the faithful in the diocese to which God has called me to shepherd."

After he hung up the telephone with the Chancellor, Sean stood and looked around the living room of his condo. The candles had all burned down. The incense burner was devoid of incense. Sean walked around the room blowing out the candles. Then he just stood looking at the prayer desk and the crucifix that had been the center of his focus for the past few hours. He dropped to his knees yet one more time. He lifted his hands and expressed his gratitude to God. He prayed that the Almighty would help him be a good and faithful bishop. Then his mind was silent. He lowered his face into his hands and closed his eyes. He knelt in the stillness. The ringing of the telephone brought him back to reality.

"Hello."

"Is this The Reverend Canon Sean Evans?"

"Yes."

"Canon Evans, will you please remain on the line for the Presiding Bishop?"

Sean felt his knees go weak. He sat down and waited to hear the voice of the Presiding Bishop of the Episcopal Church.

After receiving congratulations from the Presiding Bishop, Sean received yet one more telephone call. This one surprised him. It was from Horace Drummond. Horace was gracious in his congratulations. He assured Sean that the fact that he had also been a candidate for the position would not be a problem. Clearly the Holy Spirit had called on Sean to be the bishop and he looked forward to working with him. Horace reassured Sean. "You are now my bishop. You will have my devotion, my loyalty, and my obedience." None of the other candidates called Sean. Over the next couple of days he tried to call each one of them but none of them accepted his calls.

Sean called his own bishop to advise him of his election. His bishop told him that he was coming over and that some of the diocesan staff would be coming with him. When they arrived there were hugs, smiles, tears and congratulations. The bishop began pouring wine for all of them. He showed Sean the label. It read "Bishop Wine—Cabernet Sauvignon."

Once the wine was consumed, the bishop and staff once again left Sean to the silence. It was a holy silence. Sean had never been happier in his life. He stretched out on the couch thinking that he'd just relax and enjoy the moment. Then his doorbell rang. When he opened it, Jim Vernon collected him in his arms and passionately kissed him on the lips. He held Sean's face in his hands and smiled, "I was afraid I wasn't going to get here. I took the last flight out of Savannah to Mobile. I could not let this day go by without seeing you." He grinned devilishly. "Now take me to your bedroom, handsome. I've never slept with a bishop."

chapter 4

"WHAT I AM hearing is that you're burned out." Bishop Powers had been listening to Steele for almost an hour.

"I may be, Bishop, but I think it's even more. I am so discouraged. Over the past couple of weeks I've started questioning whether or not I should even be a priest."

"And has it affected your marriage?"

Steele felt a lump rise up in his throat. "I need to tell you about that as well. I'm afraid I've been a real jerk. I allowed these folks to almost destroy my marriage."

Bishop Powers was quiet for a couple of minutes. "Steele, I need to ask you. Did you do something you shouldn't have done? Did you act out with another woman? I fear I've seen clergy do that more often than I care to count. They act out because they are exhausted, feeling unappreciated, lonely, oh...you name it."

"No, Bishop, I assure you that kind of stuff was the last thing on my mind." Steele hesitated. "But they'd been pretty successful in convincing me that Randi was being unfaithful."

"You really have been put through the wringer."

"Bishop, it's left me depleted. I have nightmares about the place. Sometimes, during the day, the memories of the stuff they put me through just wash over me like a tsunami. They come out of nowhere. I can't eat. I've lost so much weight I look like I have a terminal disease. I know that I'm depressed. Our family doctor has given me a prescription for that, but it doesn't seem to be helping."

"Steele, how much do you know about Post Traumatic Stress Disorder?"

"I've studied it."

"You're describing all the characteristics. Have you thought about seeing a mental health professional?"

"I have an appointment with a psychiatrist in Falls City. He doesn't go to First Church but I've met him socially and I like him."

"Sounds like a good idea to me. You know, Steele, not every con-gregation treats its priests the way they've treated you. I am kicking myself for not telling you to come back to Oklahoma when you called me the first time."

"You mean when they were failing to honor the terms of my con-tract of call and wanted to rewrite it?"

"I should have told you to call up the moving van and come home right then. When a person or a parish reveals who they really are the first time, we need to believe them. They are not going to change. Those people showed you their true colors from the start. They are mean, cheap and shallow."

"Wow, Bishop, that's harsh, especially coming from you."

"I apologize. I guess I'm just getting pretty angry about the way you've been treated. You know Steele, we've talked about this before, but you are a very trusting person. Perhaps you're just a bit too trust-ing. When you combine a trusting spirit with a dose of naive you have a combination that mean folks like to use to their advantage."

"I guess that's all the more reason I shouldn't be a priest. I'd rath-er trust than not trust. If I have to stop looking for the best in people in order to be a priest, then I don't want to be one anymore."

"No, you don't have to change who you are in order to be a faith-ful priest. You just need to remember what so many of us forget in the Church. All of us are sinners. There's a reason that we have a confes-sion in the service every Sunday. "

"I just don't know anymore. Do you think I should spend the next few months exploring other career opportunities? I've got a friend in Oklahoma City that tried to get me to go into real estate before I moved to Falls City. I've been thinking that I should telephone her and see if the offer is still open."

"Steele, from the first time that I met you, I discerned that God had his hand on you. I still believe that. I believe the Lord wants you to be a priest. I fear that all you've been through has caused you to question that."

"I just don't feel the excitement for ministry any longer. The only thing I know for certain at this moment is that going back to First Church is the last thing I want to do. I don't even want to drive past the property. I want to put my hands over my ears when anyone tries to tell me anything about that place."

"That's all very understandable."

"There's more."

Steele could hear the Bishop lighting a cigarette. That was the one bad habit he possessed. He was a chain smoker, but beyond that Steele believed Bishop Powers was close to perfect. He heard the Bishop exhale the smoke from his lungs. "Talk to me."

"Bishop, I don't want to go to any church. I try to pray, but I can't. I don't even want to listen to inspirational music. I feel like I'm dead on the inside."

"Steele, listen to me." Bishop Power's voice was filled with empathy. "The flashbacks and nightmares are all symptomatic of PTSD. The emotional disconnect you're experiencing is also indicative of that affliction. Emotionally, you've been drained. Disengaging from the source of your trauma is the mind's way of coping. The apathy you feel is to be expected. I'm beginning to think it's a critical part of your healing."

"Gosh, that all makes a lot of sense. I've just not had an opportunity to talk with my shrink about it."

"Steele, you're one of my boys. Personally, I am very proud of what you've been able to accomplish in Falls City. You are a rising star in the Episcopal Church and if some of the folks at First Church can't see it, then they're even dumber than I now think they are."

"Thanks, Bishop, but I fear I really don't care what they think or don't think. I just don't care anymore."

"Steele, I want to make sure you follow through with the psychiatrist because I believe he can help you with your PTSD. That's his area of expertise. But I want to help you with the crisis of faith that this experience has produced in you."

"Bishop, I don't think I am having a crisis of faith. I still believe in God. I still believe in the Gospel story. It's the Church that I don't want anything to do with right now."

"I understand." The bishop was quiet for a moment. "Steele, have you ever heard of Pawleys Island in South Carolina?"

"I've heard of it. It's somewhere close to Charleston, I think. Randi and I had a wonderful weekend in Charleston a few years ago."

"That's right. It's just north of Charleston."

"Why do you ask?"

"An oilman in the diocese has a house there that he's offered to me for the next month. I plan to take him up on it and spend the month there. I'd like to check to see if he knows someone that just might have another house that you and Randi could use for the same time. Would you be interested?"

"I'd have to ask Randi, but I have a hunch she'd want to go. The only thing we've planned for my sabbatical is to spend some time with each set of grandparents and stay as far away from First Church as is humanly possible."

"Great, I'll make a telephone call and get back to you. It will afford us some time to have some lengthy conversations. I'd really like to help you through all this. Steele, you're a good priest. You just need to believe in yourself again."

"Thanks, Bishop, but I'm just not as sure of that as you seem to be."

"Steele, at your service of ordination did you want me to ordain you to be a priest?"

"With all my heart."

"Did you believe God had called you to be a priest?"

"There was not a doubt in my mind."

"Do you believe God made a mistake?"

"No, Bishop, I don't believe God makes mistakes, but I'm beginning to wonder if I have."

"Then that's what we need to talk about. We'll have every day for the next month to do that very thing. God bless you, Steele. Hug Randi and those beautiful children for me. I am going to be praying for you. If it all works out I'll see you and your family on the beach at Pawleys Island in a few days."

chapter 5

THE RIGHT REVEREND Rufus Petersen was in the process of packing up his office. He would no longer be the Bishop of the Diocese of Savannah. Rufus had known that he wanted to be a bishop from the day that he was first ordained a deacon in the Church. He had strategically planned every relationship and every job in his career to position himself as the perfect candidate for the office. He knew that he'd not won his election to the episcopate fairly. His predecessor had pretty much manipulated the election process, but that didn't matter to him. What mattered was that he had become a bishop. Now, as he and his longtime secretary dismantled his office, he was amazed that he actually felt nothing. There was no sadness in the process but then there was no joy either. He was simply going through the motions. He couldn't say the same for his secretary.

Big tears were rolling down her black face. "Will you please stop that!" He shouted.

"I'sa can't help it, Bishop." She blubbered. "It's just so sad. My heart is torn to pieces. I'm a gonna miss you somethin' awful."

Rufus had hired her in a nod to political correctness. She had grown on him. She'd most likely saved his life when he had his heart attack. She had a lip on her and would argue with him at the drop of a hat. He had actually grown to enjoy her bantering. Truth was, he'd grown quite fond of her and he would miss her as well. "I should have fired you before they elected my successor."

She turned her body to face him. She wiped away her tears with her hand and then put both of her hands on her hips. "And just who would have cleaned up the mess you've left in this office?"

"There is no mess." He shot back.

Her eyes widened and she wagged her finger at him. "Now you listen here. I'm the only one that knows where all the bodies are buried, and if you want them to stay buried you'd better take your leave gently."

Rufus dismissed her remarks with a wave of his hand and went back to packing. "You can say whatever you want. After Canon Evans is ordained you'll be his problem."

"Yes suh, and he's gonna be just as lucky to have me as you've been. It grieves me to think just what a mess this place would be for that new bishop if I hadn't been here to pick up after you."

"Go get us a Co-cola and make us a snack. Let's sit down and take a little break." With that Rufus sat down in the chair behind his desk. His secretary left to go get the drinks and see what was in the staff kitchen they could eat. His mind went to the very last meeting he had here just last week. At the insistence of Stone Clemons and Chief Sparks from First Church he'd summoned Ned Boone, Elmer and Judith Idle to his office. The five of them had sat in chairs like recalcitrant children facing him. Rufus did not like Stone Clemons. Stone had opposed him and his every program since he'd become bishop. He was quite aware that the bitter taste was mutual. But on this occasion the two men were united.

"Mister Clemons and Chief Sparks here have made some very serious allegations against the three of you. They have shown me pictures and correspondence from you, Mister Boone, which quite frankly make me sick to my stomach. You deliberately put one of my priest's wives in a compromising position. Then you took photographs of her and sent them to her husband. Not only did you attempt to destroy one of my priests, but you attempted to destroy his marriage."

"Ned was only doing what was in the best interest of our church!" Elmer Idle barked.

"Now you sit there and keep your mouth shut, Mister Idle. You are not being helpful. I will be getting to the two of you in a few minutes."

"I don't have to sit here and listen to you talk to me like that." Elmer started to stand.

Rufus Petersen rose from his chair and leaned across his desk. He pointed his finger directly into Elmer's face. "You will sit there and you will keep your mouth closed even if I have to get Mister Clemons and the Chief here to restrain you. Do I make myself clear!" Elmer sank back in his chair.

"Mister Boone, do you have any explanation for what you tried to do to Father Austin and his wife?"

"Bishop, we thought you understood. We've talked to you about all of this before. Steele Austin is destroying First Church. We're desperate. We need him to go. I did what I did because I thought it was the best thing for our beloved parish. The man is a train wreck."

"And in your mind destroying that priest's marriage was a charitable approach to the situation."

"I did what I felt needed to be done and I'd do it all again if I thought it would work."

"That's the part that bothers me," Rufus reflected.

"If you want to come down on anybody you ought to come down on those two." Ned pointed at Stone and the Chief. "They, along with the rest of the band of thieves on the vestry, have given Austin a six-month paid vacation. Is that the way this diocese rewards incompetence?"

"Mister Boone, it bothers me that you don't realize that you have so broken the spirit of one of my priests and so put his marriage in jeopardy that they just may be beyond repair. I detect no remorse in you for what you've done."

"I have done nothing to be sorry for. I have no regrets. Bishop, I tried to do what you obviously did not have the courage to do. I tried to get rid of a sorry excuse for a priest and save our church."

"I just don't understand why you aren't thanking Ned for what he's done." Elmer Idle whispered.

Rufus Petersen glared at him. "Now, Mister Idle, let's consider your actions. Not only have you and your wife been co-conspirators with Mister Boone in his efforts to destroy one of my priests, but you, sir, manipulated the election of a bishop."

Elmer shook his head. "I don't know what you're talking about.

"Did you or did you not call Horace Drummond in the process of the election and advise him that he was not getting any votes when, in fact, he was the leading candidate?"

Elmer looked over at Ned. Then he shrugged his shoulders.

"Mister Idle, you and I both know that was a lie. If the election process had played out, Doctor Drummond would have been elected and we all know it."

"It's bad enough we have one of them on our staff at First Church; we sure as hell don't need one for a bishop!" Ned Boone blurted.

The bishop shot him an angry look. "I am not even going to dignify that statement with a response." The bishop turned again to look at Elmer. "Mister Idle, I am going to ask you one more time. Did you or did you not call Doctor Drummond and lie to him about the number of votes he was getting?"

Elmer stared down at the floor. Rufus Petersen rose from his seat yet one more time and slammed his hand down on his desk so hard that everyone nearly jumped from their seats. The Chief and Stone were equally startled. "Answer me!"

Elmer looked over at Ned. "Yes, but it was your Canon, Jim Vernon, that came up with the idea. He was behind the entire thing."

The bishop sat back in his chair and threw his hands up in the air. He looked over at Stone and Chief Sparks and let out a sigh of exasperation. "So that's your defense. You want to blame someone else."

"But it's true. Ned and Judith can tell you that's the way it was."

"Let me tell you what I know to be true. I know that it was you and not Jim Vernon that called Doctor Drummond. I know that it was you that told my Canon that Doctor Drummond had withdrawn. My Canon merely relayed the message to me."

Judith whimpered, "But it was all his idea."

"Prove it."

The three of them looked at each other. Then Ned brightened, "I have lunch receipts from when we met with him to plan the entire thing."

"I know about those lunches. My Canon reported to me each time he met with you. He told me that he was trying to get the three of you to be more supportive of the rector. He was especially concerned about you, Judith."

"Me? Why me?"

"Because you were an employee of the rector. We just can't have staff members undermining the rectors in this diocese. You should have given your loyalty to your rector or resigned. Insubordination is not acceptable."

Ned's voice rose in anger. "Well, you're going to have to choose, Bishop. Are you going to believe us or the man that really did mastermind this election?"

Bishop Petersen smiled and then winked at the Chief and Stone, both of whom had been silent throughout the entire confrontation. "Let me see. I can believe my Canon who has never lied to me and has kept me informed of his every move. Or I can believe three people who tried to destroy a priest and his wife and lied to the man that should be sitting in this chair after me. Tough choice."

Ned stood. "You believe what you want to believe. Come on, Elmer and Judith. We don't have to listen to any more of this."

The Bishop stood. "Before you go I need to give you something." He handed each of them a sheet of paper.

"What is this?"

"These are your Letters of Transfer. You are no longer members of First Church. I've left the parish you're transferring to blank. You can take this document to any parish in my diocese and you will be welcomed, but you are not to return to First Church."

"And if we do?"

"Then I am leaving instructions to have the next bishop excommunicate you and you will no longer be members of the Episcopal Church. I am also instructing Stone Clemons and the Chief here to report the details of this meeting to the vestry and leaders of First Church. If you dare to return to First Church, I am instructing them to go into the pulpit and report the details of this meeting to the entire congregation. Now unless you want the details of what you've done made public, and perhaps even an item for the media outlets, I suggest you find a quiet little congregation and behave yourselves." The bishop then dismissed them with a wave of his hand. "Now get out of my sight. Go! Go!"

"What are you thinkin' so hard about, Bishop?" His secretary had returned with Co-Colas and snacks. She sat them down on the desk and took a seat opposite him.

"I was just remembering that meeting last week."

Her eyes brightened and she nodded her head. "You mean the one with those troublemakers from First Church?"

"That's the one."

A broad smile crossed her face. "You know that meeting stirred up some strange feelings in my heart."

"What do you mean? You weren't there."

She threw back her head and enjoyed a laugh that shook her entire body. "How long I been yor secretary?"

"I don't know…years I guess."

"And you think that there was anything going on in this office I didn't hear?"

Rufus looked around his office. "How? You got my office bugged?"

She couldn't contain her laughter. Tears began rolling down her cheeks once again. "Oh, Bishop, I don't need no bugs. I got my own way doin' things."

"Well, I need to warn Canon Evans."

"You go right ahead and do that. Let's just see if he's any smarter than you."

Rufus shook his head in exasperation. "I should have fired you."

She took a sip of her drink. "You know what I thought after that meeting when I saw them folks leave here with their tails between their legs?"

"Go on."

"I thought…my, oh my…Rufus has finally become a bishop. It's just a shame he come to it at quit'n time."

"What do you mean?"

"I don't know much about being a bishop and working for you all these years hasn't helped with that much, but they all call you the chief shepherd of the diocese, right?"

"That's right."

"Well, isn't the chief shepherd supposed to protect the other shepherds from the wolves?"

"I never thought of it that way."

"Well, I been workin' in this office just long enough to figure out that sometimes them wolves are dressed in sheep clothing."

Rufus put his sandwich down and looked at her for a long moment. She stared back at him. "If you repeat this to anyone I'll swear it's a lie, but you know what?"

"What?"

"I think I am really going to miss you."

With that she rose from her chair and went around to his side of the desk. He rose and put his hands up in front of him. "Now don't you hug me. I told you when you went to work for me there would be no hugging."

She ignored him and wrapped her arms around him as he tried to wiggle away. Then he relaxed into her embrace and put his arms around her. Their tears mingled as they dropped onto one another's face.

⁕

chapter 6

VIRGINIA MUDD WAS on her fourth glass of sweet tea and it wasn't even noon. Her therapy group would meet at one o'clock. She just needed to hang on until then. The thing that she wanted to do most was to go over to Alicia's house. She had been Virginia's truest friend in this town. She had covered for her with Henry when she was having an affair with Jacque. Even now she felt a tingling when she thought of Jacque. They had spent so many passionate afternoons naked in bed at Alicia's lake house. There they smoked joint after joint and made love multiple times. It would be so nice if she could just go over to Alicia's, smoke a joint or two, drink some wine and then she could go out and get herself laid. The touch of a strange man so excited her.

Virginia looked around the two-room duplex she now called home. She had fallen so far from the big house on River Street that she used to preside over. She had been one of the stars of Falls City society. She had been Mrs. Henry Mudd. She hadn't been completely dependent on Henry for her position or wealth. Her parents were well situated in the society of Falls City. The prayer desks at First Church were dedicated to their memory. When they died they'd actually left her a substantial trust filled with stocks, bonds and real estate holdings. Through the years, however, she'd managed to cash them in and sell the income properties. Now she had none of it left. She could just kick herself for that. The real sadness is that she had nothing to show for the money. The few pieces of jewelry and a closet full of shoes really didn't serve her. Now she was faced with selling even more of her jewelry.

Virginia lit another cigarette. It was the one habit that she'd not been able to give up. Her sponsor had allowed her to keep that one addiction. But then again, both he and her therapist were smokers. In fact, most everyone in her therapy group and her Sex Addicts Anonymous Group were smokers. There were some fringe benefits to abstaining from pot and alcohol. She was now back to the dress size she wore in her twenties. All the fad diets hadn't worked. She'd lose some weight and then gain it back and then some. Her group had finally convinced her to use one of those sensible eating programs combined with a twenty-minute walk each day. She was amazed at how quickly the weight dropped off her. Even if she said so herself, she thought she looked good.

Virginia had to distance herself from Alicia. Her therapist, sponsor, and the members of both her support groups had convinced her that Alicia was a bad influence. That was so hard for her to do. Alicia had been there for her when she had Jacque's baby aborted. She'd been there for her through all her travails. But she knew they were right. Alicia was her door to opportunity. She knew that if she were to see her again she would quickly fall back into her old ways.

Henry had driven a hard if not cruel settlement in their divorce. The settlement package she'd agreed to did not last long. She was being very frugal but she knew the time was coming when she'd have to get a job. The problem was that she really had no skills. She guessed that she could work in retail. That would be acceptable. Waitressing was out of the question. As low as she'd fallen, she knew she just couldn't do that.

The clock indicated that she still had another hour to wait before she could leave for her therapy group. Her anonymous group meetings and her therapy group were the only thing sustaining her. She lived for these gatherings. Just hearing the stories of other addict's struggles with temptation helped her combat her own. Her sponsor was wonderful. He was always just a telephone call away. She called him often. She thought he would probably be even better help if he weren't so damn handsome. He had long coal black hair. His eyes were so dark she was convinced she could literally get lost in them. He had broad shoulders and a hard chest with a tiny little waist. His bottom looked next to perfect in the tight jeans he insisted on wearing to the meetings. "Oh my God, I'd like to pull those jeans off him and ride him like he was a stallion in a fox hunt." Virginia snickered. "I can't believe I just said that out loud." She got up to get herself another glass of sweet tea. "Maybe this will help calm me down. I've just got to stop thinking about him like that."

Virginia walked out onto her tiny little front porch. She sat down in the rocker she'd placed there and lit another cigarette. She reasoned that she'd made some good progress with her recovery program. She'd not smoked a joint, had any alcohol, or sex with a man in almost six months now. She was working her steps and attending the meetings. When temptation overwhelmed her she called her sponsor. "God, every time I think about that man I get horny." She held the iced tea glass to her forehead. "Maybe I should get another sponsor."

She'd even found a new church to attend. That had surprised her. Her ancestors came to this country from England. They belonged to the Church of England. She was a fifth generation Episcopalian. She never dreamed that she would ever be anything else. But she'd accepted the fact that she'd never be able to return to First Church. That church, the country club, the Magnolia Club, the women's club, the Junior League was all now but a distant memory for her. She did still hope her daughters would make their debut and be presented to society. She'd want to be there for that. She'd have to swallow what little pride she had left on those occasions.

Virginia had found her new church through the other members of the group. It was a community church over on the north side of the city. There were lots of new houses being built over there and this church had bought up a lot of property. They had a huge campus with a school, a day care center, a gymnasium, and a monstrous worship center that looked more like a basketball arena than a church. It was a different kind of worship experience for her. They didn't have a pipe organ but they did have a band that played jubilant music to get the service started. The place was packed on Sundays but Virginia was safe. She was certain that not a single person from her former life would be caught dead in her new congregation, and so far she'd been right.

The minister didn't preach so much about Jesus or the Gospels as he motivated folks to believe in themselves. Virginia liked his messages of personal affirmation. They had touched her life. She could tell by the tears streaming down the faces of the people around her that the messages were important to others as well. Virginia figured that most everyone that was in her two groups attended this church. She saw so many people from the various groups that met the same nights that her group met. There were recovering alcoholics, gamblers, and drug addicts all present at the services. She'd even thought that they should change their name from Community Church to the Church of the Anonymous.

Virginia went back into the house so that she could look at the clock. Another thirty minutes and she could leave for the meeting. Her eyes fell on the picture of her two daughters. They'd been so angry with her. Henry said that they'd been subjected to some cruel teasing at First Church School. The kids had taunted them, telling them that their mother was a slut. The boys had tried to put the move on her oldest daughter. *Your mother puts out so why don't you?* Her daughters had just barely talked to her over the past few months. Tears welled up in her eyes as she thought about what she'd done to them. Maybe that's what she needed to talk about in today's session.

Henry had not spoken to her in several weeks now. Any communication she'd had with the girls had been through Shady. At one time Shady had been her childhood playmate. Then she'd become her *Help*. When she called the house, Shady was still civil and respectful to Virginia, but there was something in her voice that let her know that she disapproved of the choices she'd made.

Virginia went into her tiny bathroom to freshen up before she left for the group therapy session. She critiqued the reflection in her mirror. Henry used to tell her she was pretty. Jacque, one of her many lovers, repeatedly tried to reassure her that she was beautiful. Virginia wanted to believe all of them. She just didn't see it for herself. The mirror only confirmed her many imperfections. Still it seemed to fill an empty spot in her life when she was complimented on her looks. In social situations she recognized that she went out of her way to gain the attention of a handsome man. There were times she felt desperate to hear a flattering remark. When one was given she would delight in it for days. If the compliments were generous enough, Virginia would reward the giver the only way she knew how. She loved seeing the look of pleasure on a man's face. Her pleasure was the knowledge that she had made that look possible.

Virginia glanced at the clock on the bedside table. She needed to hurry. The makeup would have to cover her several facial flaws. She wanted to be noticed when she entered the room. She especially enjoyed seeing the appreciative looks on the faces of the men in the group. She hoped there would be those same looks when she walked into the meeting today. Perhaps there would even be a compliment or two.

Today she knew she needed to share with the group. Virginia began to rehearse her thoughts. She would begin by telling her therapist and the others in the group that she'd been faithful to her program. She would be honest with them. She would tell them that more than anything in the world she wished she could smoke a joint, get drunk and feel the touch of a naked stranger. She'd tell them that she had resisted those temptations and removed them from her mind as quickly as they'd entered. She'd even confess that the thought of her sponsor aroused her desire. Virginia put both of her hands down on her washbasin and stared in the mirror. No, she wouldn't tell them that. They would tell her that she had to get a new sponsor. No, she wasn't ready to do that. Not yet.

chapter 7

SEAN EVANS WAS now the Bishop Elect of the Diocese of Savannah. Things were really falling into place for him. He'd placed his condo on the market and the very first person to look at it on the first day it was listed made a cash offer. They wanted to take possession within thirty days. That was perfect. Sean had started packing up his personal things for the move to Savannah. He'd planned to go up to Savannah the coming weekend to find a condo or perhaps a house that he could buy.

The front doorbell rang and Sean answered. A delivery service had a package for him. He knew exactly what it was. He opened the package with eagerness. Inside were three clergy shirts all in the colors worn by bishops. He had spent hours considering the shirts in the *Bishop's Catalog* from the ecclesiastical garment company. He simply couldn't decide which color to order. He'd ordered one shirt in each of the three colors he'd seen bishops wear. He'd decided to try each one on and then choose the color that he thought looked best on him.

The first shirt he tried on was a bright maroon. It was almost red. He looked at himself in the mirror. With his skin complexion and hair color he just didn't think that one flattered him at all.

He tried on the deep purple shirt next. Now that was better, but he still thought that perhaps it would look better on a person with a dark complexion. Even with his tan, he just didn't think that this one was his best choice.

The last shirt was the color that he'd seen most bishops wear. It was a lighter shade of maroon. Even before he buttoned it up he knew that would be his choice. Perhaps he should wait and see what Jim Vernon thought. After all, Jim did have impeccable taste in clothing. Jim had been his lover on and off for years. Now that they would be working together maybe he should ask him before making a final decision.

Sean turned back to one of the boxes he'd been packing. He was going to have to see just where his relationship with Jim was going to go. It could get complicated. Over the past few years they'd lived in separate cities in separate states. They talked on the telephone often and had taken several trips together. When they were together they couldn't keep their hands off each other. But it was all in controlled situations. After the week or weekend they'd each return to their separate lives and their separate ministries. Now things were going to be different.

Hunger sounds growling in his stomach interrupted his thoughts. He went out to the kitchen and retrieved a protein shake from the refrigerator. He sat down at his kitchen table in order to think this new situation through just a bit further.

He pulled out the picture of Jim that he carried in his wallet so he could look at it. Jim was one handsome fellow. He had a solid build and he worked hard at staying in shape. Sean appreciated that about him. They always enjoyed each other's company. They had fun together both in and out of bed. Jim was Sean's best friend. He loved him. He just didn't know if he was *in love* with him.

As bishop, he would have to give Jim instructions. He would be in charge of his ministry schedule. He would be signing Jim's checks and determining whether or not he was to receive increases in salary. That could really complicate things. But then living in the same city and working in the same office could really be nice. They could steal a few minutes with each other in the middle of the day. The ringing of the telephone interrupted his thoughts. Sean chuckled. "Wouldn't it be funny if it was Jim on the line?" He thought about answering the telephone, "Bishop Evans", but decided against it.

"Hello, Sean Evans here."

"Canon Evans, this is Bishop North, John North. I am the Bishop in charge of the Office of Pastoral Development for the Presiding Bishop."

"Yes, Bishop North, I know you. We met at General Convention last year. It's nice to hear your voice. Thanks for calling."

"Canon Evans, this is not a courtesy call. It's the kind of call I don't like to make, but circumstances require me to do so."

"Well, that sounds rather ominous."

Canon Evans...may I call you Sean?"

"Yes, please do."

"Thank you. I'd prefer it if you called me John."

"Okay. What's this all about, John?"

"Sean, I fear that we have a problem."

"What kind of problem?"

"An accusation of sexual misconduct has been made against you."

"A what?" Panic rose up in Sean's stomach.

"Yes, my office received a telephone call from an attorney in your diocese that claims that one of her clients insists that you made inappropriate advances."

"Excuse me, John, but that's just bullshit."

"Sean, I hope that you understand that we have to investigate this. Until this is resolved, the process for consecrating you a bishop must be placed on hold."

"What does that mean?"

"Just what I said. Unless we can resolve these accusations in your favor, your election as the Bishop of Savannah will be revoked."

"Now let me get this straight. Because someone claims I made inappropriate advances my election could be revoked."

"I fear so."

"John, I can't believe this. I've sold my condo. I've resigned my job. I am packed up to move to Savannah and one phone call could leave me unemployed and homeless. That's just crap."

"Sean, I understand that this is upsetting for you, but it has to be resolved."

"What is the name of the person accusing me?"

"All of that will be revealed to you in due time. Right now we have to take these accusations seriously. The attorney says that if we proceed to make you a bishop, her client will come to your consecration and disrupt the service by making their accusation public at the allotted time in the service."

"What do we do? How do I go about proving that they are lying?"

"I need you to be here in my office in New York on Monday. Let's say two o'clock. Can you do that?"

"Of course. I'll be there."

"Until then, Sean, I suggest that you mention this to no one."

"I was going to Savannah this weekend to buy a place to live."

"I wouldn't do that if I were you. You may not be moving to Savannah. Until we get this resolved, you must not think of yourself as a bishop elect."

"You mean I could literally end up with no job and no home because of one crazy person's accusation."

"Sean, I know this is difficult, but the attorney has reported the accusation and it has to be investigated. I will see you on Monday and we'll have a look at the facts."

Both rage and nausea rushed through Sean's body as he hung up the telephone. This simply couldn't be happening. He racked his memory trying to think just who might have accused him. Then it hit him. He'd just assumed that the accusation was coming from some fag he'd offended. Maybe it was coming from another priest that was jealous of his election and simply wanted to out him. He hadn't even asked Bishop North if his accuser was a man or a woman. He'd never put a move on any woman. He simply wasn't interested. For a moment Sean relaxed. He hoped it was a woman. He could easily disprove that. He knew what he was going to have to tell John North on Monday if it did turn out that his accuser was a woman. It was the only way he knew that he could absolutely disprove that kind of accusation. But would it hurt or help? Either way could be his undoing. His dream of becoming a bishop could come smashing to the floor on Monday.

chapter 8

"AREN'T THEY HAVING services at First Church this Sunday?" Harlan McMurray stretched out his hand to Ned Boone. He then shook Elmer Idle's hand and gave Judith Idle a broad smile. The three returned his welcome.

"I don't ever plan to darken the door of First Church again." Ned Boone barked.

A puzzled look crossed Harlan's face. "I thought you were one of the cornerstones over there, Ned. Elmer, aren't you on the vestry?" His puzzled expression then focused on Judith. "I thought you were on the staff of First Church. What's going on?"

"Ned speaks for Judith and me as well. None of us want anything else to do with that place."

Judith put her hand on her husband's arm. "Now, Elmer, you know that we own plots in the First Church Cemetery, so we'll have to go over there at least one more time."

Ned groaned. "Yeah, but the best part is that you won't know it."

Harlan's puzzled expression grew even more intense. "You all need to explain this to me. I just don't understand."

"What's to understand, Harlan?" Ned smirked. "First Church has gone to hell in a hand basket under Steele Austin. We've simply taken all that we can stand. You'd better get ready. There's going to be a mass exit. We expect hundreds of members at First Church to follow us out of that place. Many of them are going to end up right here at Saint Andrew's Presbyterian."

Harlan nodded, "I'd heard rumors on the cocktail circuit that some of the membership has not been happy with your rector but I thought that had all changed."

Judith wiped away the tear rolling down her cheek. "We have all prayed that it would not end like this."

Harlan's expression changed from perplexed to concerned. "Judith, are you okay?"

"None of us like what's happened over there." Elmer said with disgust in his voice. "It's broken all of our hearts. We loved that church. We've given our lives for it. We've sacrificed our time and money to see that God's will is done in that place, but I fear that Satan has won the battle."

"I am so sorry to hear this." Harlan nodded. "But you are going to have to give me more. I just don't understand what could have happened to cause you all to leave the parish that has been at the center of your lives."

"I wish I could point to just one thing," Ned struggled to explain. "It's the culmination of so many things. The bottom line is that we just can't support the rector any longer. We find everything from his leadership style to his so-called spirituality to be objectionable."

Again, Harlan nodded. "I am so sorry. Was there one thing in particular that made you decide to leave?"

The words shot out of Elmer's mouth. "They've given that poor excuse for a priest a six-month paid vacation! Can you believe that? The man works part time as it is. That hothead, Steele Austin, shot off his mouth at a meeting of the vestry and then walked out. After losing his temper and using a cuss word in the meeting, they've rewarded him by giving him a six-month vacation. Have you ever heard of such a thing? Can you believe they're going to pay him to do nothing for the next six months? I've never gotten a six-month paid vacation in my life. I seriously doubt if any of us have, but the bleeding hearts in his fan club over there have rewarded his poor performance with what they're calling a sabbatical."

"How long has he been there?" Harlan asked.

"Not long enough to earn that kind of benefit at the membership's expense." Elmer's face grew red with anger. "The quality of his work alone would have gotten him fired in the corporate world."

"I only asked because our minister got a six-month sabbatical a couple of years ago, but he'd been here over ten years so the board decided to give him one."

"How do you like your minister?" Ned Boone asked.

Harlan motioned for them to come closer. He looked around to see if anyone was listening. Then he whispered, "Well to tell you the truth, there are quite a few of us that think he has been here long enough. We think his time has come."

Judith looked disappointed. "Oh, I thought he was a true man of God. I know that several of my friends that belong to this parish are really devoted to him."

"He has them fooled." Harlan spit the words from his mouth. "But he doesn't have me fooled and doesn't have some of the powerful people in this parish fooled."

"I understand that he's a pretty good preacher." Elmer looked puzzled.

"Well, it's time for the service to begin. Come on in and see for yourself. Will you all sit with me?"

The trio followed Harlan into St. Andrew's Presbyterian Church. The sanctuary of St. Andrew's Church was cavernous by comparison to First Church. There was only one service on Sunday morning versus the multiple services held at First Church. That alone necessitated the larger seating capacity. However, St. Andrew's was often seen as a feeder parish for First Church. The membership of St. Andrew's was made up of middle management and upper class blue-collar folks. There were a few aristocrats of Scottish descent at St. Andrew's. Their loyalty to the Presbyterian denomination and St. Andrew's in particular had more to do with their loyalty to the homeland than anything else. They would never consider being members of First Church. As the middle management folks at Saint Andrews increased their wealth and social position they would transfer their membership to First Church soon after being accepted as members of the country club.

The sanctuary was lined with white pews trimmed with dark wood. The choir spread out behind the pulpit that was at the center of the front platform. There were no stained glass windows but some very large brass and crystal chandeliers hung from the ceiling. Judith Idle began to miss some of the things about the Episcopal Church immediately. There was no procession of the cross, choir and clergy. She missed seeing the altar. She missed the stained glass. She missed having kneelers in the pews. There was no Book of Common Prayer. But most of all she missed her friends at First Church. There she was a person of note. As a spiritual leader she was given admiration and adulation. She felt so alone in this new church. Tears welled up in her eyes.

The senior minister entered wearing a robe that looked like he was at the commencement service for a university. In a deep baritone voice he called the congregation to worship. Everyone stood and sang a hymn. An assistant pastor offered a short prayer. He then asked the congregation to be seated. The assistant pastor welcomed all the visitors and encouraged everyone to turn and greet the people sitting around them. Another minister read a scripture lesson. Then the senior minister asked all to stand while he offered the pastoral prayer that continued for what seemed like ten minutes. He prayed for the President, the Vice President, the Supreme Court, the Congress, the Governor and the legislation, the Mayor of the city and the council, the military, the ministers, the choir, the Sunday school, and the sick and dying. Then he started giving thanks for all God's blessings from the beauty of nature to his own good health. Ned whispered to Elmer, "He prays longer than Austin preaches." The two men snickered.

After the morning offering was received and the choir had offered the anthem, the senior minister preached the morning message. The trio from First Church grew restless as the sermon passed the thirty-minute mark. They simply weren't used to sitting for that long of a stretch in church. After the closing hymn, Harlan turned to the three of them and asked, "Well, what did you think?"

Ned gently shook his head. "He sure has a lot to say. I just didn't think he was going to try to say it all in one sermon."

Harlan threw back his head and let the laughter roar out of him. "You got that right. I think he enjoys his sermons enough for all of us." The trio chuckled and nodded their agreement.

Harlan once again lowered his voice to a whisper. "Now do you understand why some of us think it's time for him to go?"

Ned nodded. "I certainly understand. Personally I don't care for him. There's just something about his holier than thou air I find objectionable."

Harlan put his hand on Ned's arm. "Can I ask if you folks are seriously considering becoming members here at St. Andrew's?"

Ned smiled, "Only if you're serious about getting a new preacher."

"Harlan reached his hand out to shake each of their hands. "I want to be the first to welcome you to St. Andrew's. Now let's go over to the social hall. I want to introduce you to some of the other folks that feel the same way I do about removing the pastor. I hope I'll be able to count on you to help us. We need to do it for the sake of our parish."

Ned frowned, "Let me ask you one question."

"Yes."

"Will you have to get a bishop's permission to remove him or can the leaders of the congregation do it?"

Harlan snickered, "We leave bishops to you Episcopalians. We Presbyterians don't want anything to do with that nonsense. Our congregations are self-governing. We do whatever we want to do."

Ned, Elmer and Judith all smiled.

❧

chapter 9

"HORACE, MAY I have a word with you?" Stone Clemons walked into the priest's sacristy. The Reverend Doctor Horace Drummond was preparing to lead the nine o'clock service.

"Sure, Stone. What can I do for you?"

"Have you received any reports of the gossip on the First Church cocktail circuit?"

Horace's baritone chuckle filled the little room. "There's always gossip on the cocktail circuit. You're going to have to be more specific."

Stone smiled and nodded. "Guess you're right about that."

"I take it there's some particular misinformation being passed around that you want to address."

"Well, actually I was hoping you might address a couple of issues this morning."

"I'd like to try, but I already have my sermon prepared."

"Oh, I'm not suggesting that you rewrite your sermon. I just think that perhaps a few words on a couple of subjects could go a long way toward putting some oil on the congregational water."

"Go on."

"You've heard the talk that Steele won't be coming back. "

Horace nodded. "I've heard. A couple of folks asked me about it. I tried to reassure them."

"I think a few words from the pulpit might help."

"Okay. No problem."

"There's more." Stone grimaced. "There's the ugly rumor that Steele and Randi are separated and he's filing for a divorce."

"Whoa! I hadn't heard that one. That's just mean. I'll take care of that one post haste."

Stone stood in the sacristy studying Horace's face. "There's more."

"More?"

"The vestry is getting a lot of heat for giving Steele this sabbatical. I fear that some of the people just don't understand why we did it. And…"

"And, what?"

Stone shook his head. "Frankly, I think some of the more small-minded out there are just envious. They've never had a six-month paid vacation, as they're calling it, and they're jealous that we've given one to Steele."

Horace nodded. "It could be envy and it could also be fear. Fear that they won't be taken care of in his absence. Fear that he will abandon them. And then I am sure there's some envy."

"Do you think you can say something to help?"

"I'll give it my best effort, but Stone, you and I both know that there's just no way to make some of these folks happy. They don't understand because they don't want to understand."

Stone patted Horace on the back. "You're a good man. I have every confidence in you. I believe First Church is in good hands while Steele is away."

"Now, may I ask you something?"

Stone smiled. "Anything you want."

"Do you think Steele is going to come back?"

Stone turned his head to stare at the stained glass sacristy window. It was as though he was looking for an answer to appear in the glass. After a long silence he looked back at Horace. "Selfishly, I want him to come back. There's a part of me that loves him enough to hope that he won't. I'm not sure some of these vultures will ever change. Quite frankly, I simply don't know. This one I'm afraid we have to leave in the Lord's hands."

The organist played the introduction to the opening hymn just as the verger entered the sacristy. "Doctor Drummond, are you ready?"

Horace smiled at Stone and nodded. He followed the verger into the nave and took his place in the procession.

"Before I begin my sermon this morning, I'd like to say a few things about our life together while Father Austin is on sabbatical. First, it is only natural for us all to have some anxiety about our parish in the absence of the rector. Let me assure you that you are in good hands. We have a fine staff of lay and clergy folks that are committed to keeping our parish operating smoothly. Our hard working deacon assists Mother Graystone and me. Mother Graystone will continue her excellent ministry with our singles, young adults and youth. The lion's share of the ministry to our elderly and shut-in falls on the shoulders of our deacon. She, along with our Eucharistic Ministers, will insure that the Blessed Sacrament is taken to their homes and bedsides. Quite frankly, our deacon works so much behind the scenes that unless you or one of your loved ones is a recipient of her ministry, you are unaware of all that she does." The congregation responded to Horace's remarks with applause.

"To further assure you that we are in good hands, I want you to know that Bishop Petersen has made himself available to assist us at any time before he moves to his new home in Florida. In that same vein, I spoke with our bishop elect and he told me that he would make his canon, Jim Vernon, available to us at any time we should need him while Father Austin is away.

I spoke with Father Austin a few days ago. He and Randi are enjoying having some uninterrupted time together. Almeda and I were just saying at breakfast this morning that we've never known a couple so much in love." He looked over at Almeda sitting in her new seat in the transept. On hearing his words she first looked puzzled and then quickly began to smile and nod. "Steele Austin absolutely worships the ground that his beautiful wife walks on. I do believe Randi is his number one fan and supporter." Horace stopped and smiled. "And those two precious children. Have you ever? We are so blessed to have them as our rectory family." Once again the congregation responded with applause.

"The six months that Father Austin is gone will pass quickly. I fear it will pass most quickly for him. Mother Graystone and I both can tell you that the work of a rector of a parish is unending. It may very well be the only job left where a person is expected to be on duty twenty-four hours a day seven days a week. All clergy recognize that they are signing up for the hours when they are ordained. It's part of the calling. That does not change the fact that the work schedule for clergy includes those times when their congregation is at rest. Clergy work weekdays, as you all know. Clergy also work weekends when most of us are relaxing with our families. Holidays are set aside as time for family celebrations. For clergy, they are some of our most stressful work periods. Our families must celebrate without us. I've personally seen your rector come from the bedside of a dying person into a meeting on the budget. Can you imagine making such a sudden emotional shift?"

Horace stood quietly looking at the congregation. He realized that they were all listening to his every word. "Now to say that being rector of First Church is a stressful job is an understatement." A few folks in the congregation chuckled. "And if I might be so blunt, some of us have not always been as cooperative or as supportive of our rector as we should have been." Several in the congregation shuffled in their seats and gave each other knowing looks. "In just a few short years our rector has helped this congregation grow in membership. We've added staff. We've added services. We increased our stewardship. We've started several outreach ministries that literally touch the lives of thousands of people in this community every week. He's led us to accomplish all these good things for God. And after all that, he's had to make time to argue about plastic flowers in the cemetery." The congregation roared with laughter and then exploded with more applause.

"I am the acting rector. My job is to love you and take care of you and this parish until Father Austin returns. I will not be making any structural changes to the way we do ministry. I am here for you as are all the clergy and staff. We will faithfully exercise our ministries. We are going to prepare you and ourselves for Father Austin's return. When he left us a couple of weeks ago he was tired. No, he was exhausted. When he comes bouncing back into this pulpit, he is going to be rested and energized. Here's the question you need to ask yourself. Are you ready for a newly revitalized Steele Austin? As I think about it, I might recommend that we all get a little rest over the next few months. Steele Austin is going to come back into this congregation like the *Energizer Bunny* and we'd better be ready for him." Horace stopped and smiled broadly at the congregation. "Okay, you've been warned. My job this morning is finished." The congregation rose to their feet and gave him a standing ovation. Horace looked over at Stone Clemons. He smiled and nodded.

chapter 10

HENRY MUDD ROLLED over onto his back and took a deep breath. He then reached over and put his arm under Delilah's neck. He pulled her naked body next to his. "God, Dee. Every time I think it can't get any better it does. That was wonderful."

Delilah smiled and nestled her head on his chest. She ran her fingers through his chest hair. "I rather enjoyed that myself."

"Dee, do you have any idea just how much I love you?"

"If you love me only half as much as I love you, then I am happy."

Henry closed his eyes. Delilah had taught him so much about love. There was a time when he really thought he was in love with Virginia. He even felt like he was the luckiest man on earth. He had a beautiful wife and two precious daughters. They were the toast of Falls City Society. Virginia was a wonderful homemaker, a leading volunteer in First Church, and all the right charitable endeavors. Their home on River Street was immaculately maintained. Virginia was the perfect hostess for both his business and social connections.

Delilah gave a little snore. He looked over at her face. She had gone to sleep on his chest. The feel of her face on his bare chest felt wonderful. He even thought her little sleep noises were adorable. Henry knew that he was desperately in love with this woman.

His mind went back to his marriage to Virginia. He realized now they both were just playing a role. He was the perfect husband and father. She pretended to be the ideal wife and mother. Their sex life should have told him all that he needed to know. He was convinced that if he hadn't approached Virginia they would have had a sexless marriage. That certainly wasn't the case with Delilah. It was as though she couldn't get enough of him. He felt the same way about her. Sex with Virginia had been so routine. It was almost as though he had to make an appointment with her. Even then, she'd want to put it off for as long as she could. He now realized that it was just that. It was sex and nothing more. There was no exchange of love. No merging of their souls. With Virginia it was a deed that needed to be done when his libido, not hers, needed satisfying. With Delilah he craved to be close to her. He wanted to be united with her. He hurt to be one with her. Maybe that's what the Bible really means about the two becoming one flesh.

Obviously, he'd never known that with Virginia nor had she known it with him. She could not have done what she did with all those other men if she'd loved him with her heart and her body. She'd only given him her body. He didn't know whom she had given her heart to. He only knew beyond a shadow of a doubt that she'd never given it to him. He had given Delilah his heart and his body. He could not imagine wanting to give them to any one else but her. He belonged to her. She had all of him.

Henry knew that he wanted to marry Delilah, but he wanted to do it the right way. First, he wanted her to get to know his girls and he wanted his girls to know her. He felt certain that once they got to know her they could be friends. She would be the perfect stepmother. He would wait until Steele Austin returned and have him do pre-marital counseling with them. The one thing he didn't want to have happen was to have Delilah marked as the other woman that broke up his marriage. If she became so branded by the socially elite she'd never be accepted. They would snub her and worse. He loved her too much to have her treated that way. No, they would take their time. His friends and all the proper folks would get to know her. They would want him to marry her.

His daughters had gone through a rebellious stage after their mother moved out. The oldest was dressing like a character in a horror film. The youngest got so fat he was afraid she wouldn't be able to find clothes. He'd had to have a word with the Head of First Church School about the way the other kids were treating them. At first he tried to pretend that there was nothing he could do. Henry was able to convince him otherwise. Now his daughters were doing much better. They still didn't want much to do with their mother, but he was encouraging them to forgive her.

Henry had looked at engagement rings when he was in New York last week. He felt that it was a safe place for him to shop. He didn't think he could be seen shopping for an engagement ring in Falls City. He'd seen several that he thought Delilah would like. He'd come close to purchasing one of them but then had second thoughts. He wanted Delilah to help him choose her ring. He'd get her whatever she wanted. After all, she'd taught him about love. He wondered just how many people go through life and never get to experience the marriage of love and sex. He felt sorry for them. If it hadn't been for the beautiful lady sleeping on his chest, he could have been one of them. He whispered a prayer of thanksgiving to God for Delilah. He thanked God for letting him be one of the blessed people in this life that could experience the harmony of spiritual and physical love.

Delilah stirred and then opened her eyes. "Did you nap?"

"No, I wanted to watch you."

"Did I snore?"

"A couple of times, but it was so cute. You sounded like a kitten."

She lightly thumped his chest with her fist. "You're the only man I know that would think my snoring is cute."

"I think everything about you is cute."

"Well, will you always think that? I can have some bad days. I can even have bad moods. You know, we've never had a good fight."

"Dee, I don't want to fight with you. I just want to love you."

"Even when I am in a crummy mood?"

He rolled her over onto her back and kissed her on the lips. Then he started kissing her gently on her neck before starting to move down her body. "I plan to love you forever and nothing you can ever do will change that."

She put her hands on either side of his face and brought his face back up so that she could look in his eyes. There was something she needed to tell him. She was going to have to tell him soon. It could change their entire relationship. She feared that it might even be the one thing that would stop him from loving her. She started to tell him her secret but something told her the time was not yet right. For the first time in their relationship she was filled with fear. She was afraid that she could lose Henry. She could not stand to lose him, but he must know. She knew she would have to take the chance. She needed to tell him, but just not now. Delilah looked deep into his eyes. "Henry Mudd, I love you." Then she pulled his lips to hers.

chapter 11

THE CONFEDERATE HONOR Society is by far one of the most exclusive groups in Falls City. Membership is open only to those that can prove that one of their ancestors fought in the War for Southern Independence. Proof documents must be presented to the membership committee. The first document that must be presented is a copy of the discharge papers for a blood relative issued by the Confederate Army. In lieu of that, proof of pension payments to a widow is also acceptable. The applicant for membership must demonstrate beyond a shadow of a doubt that the person they are claiming as an ancestor was, in fact, a soldier in the Southern Army.

Once the military legitimacy of the claimed ancestor is established to the committee's satisfaction, the applicant must go one step further. They must present additional documentation issued by a recognized genealogical society that they are in fact a blood relative of said veteran. The Historical Press of the Confederacy publishes books on southern genealogy. The easiest and most acceptable proof of relationship is to have one's ancestral lineage listed in one of the publications. Beyond that, most all of the genealogical society documents are accepted, save those issued by The Mormon Church. Any genealogical documents coming from Salt Lake City are immediately dismissed.

The most exclusive affair hosted by the Confederate Honor Society is held annually on January 19th to honor the birth date of General Robert E. Lee. The ball is held in the Magnolia Hotel's Grand Ballroom. The ballroom is painted Confederate gray with gold drapes and other appointments in gold. A large flag of the Confederacy hangs prominently on the wall facing the entrance doors to the ballroom.

The host committee mails engraved invitations to each member. Membership in the society is not limited to the citizens of Falls City. Members come for the annual event from throughout Georgia and Alabama. The society was further honored when members of their sister chapter in Charleston, South Carolina attended their event. All attendees understand that they must RSVP promptly in order to receive tickets for the occasion. That ticket, along with having their name on the registry, is the only way they can gain entrance to the affair. Security guards dressed in Confederate uniforms are stationed in the lobby outside the grand ballroom. If a member fails to present tickets with their name printed on them and have those tickets verified against the registry of membership, they will be firmly but politely turned away.

All the men in attendance are required to wear the uniform of the Southern Army to the event. The ladies are required to wear dresses appropriate to the period. Once inside the ballroom they can match their assigned seats for dinner with the numbers on their tickets. Before dinner, black male waiters wearing the costumes of the house servants of the plantation move about the guests, receiving and then dispensing drink orders on silver trays. Black women dressed also in the servant costumes of the plantation house carry various hors d'oeuvres on silver trays for the guests to enjoy.

Hanging prominently on the wall next to the flag of the Confederacy is a life size portrait of General Robert E. Lee and his horse, Traveller. A small orchestra is on the stage beneath the confederate flag. They play music of the period during the social hour and dinner. At each event one of the history professors from the University of Virginia up in Charlottesville is invited to attend. After dinner he recites for the gathered the life story of General Lee and his many accomplishments. Once he is finished he will receive the proper amount of adulation from the membership. The orchestra then strikes up a rousing rendition of *Dixie*. All stand and sing while an army of waiters swarms into the dining room carrying silver trays with crystal champagne glasses filled with French Champagne. The President of the Society then stands below the General's portrait and offers a birthday toast. The final tribute to the General can be found the following morning in the Falls City and State Newspapers. There in the obituary column will be a picture of the General and a story commemorating his life.

This year's president of the Confederate Society is none other than First Church's self-proclaimed head usher, Colonel Mitchell. He and his wife stood at the door to the ballroom for the first part of the evening personally greeting each guest. After retrieving a bourbon and branch from one of the waiters, Colonel Mitchell walked up to Tom Barnhardt and Gary Hendricks, who were standing in a far corner of the ballroom. They were obviously in a deep discussion. "This is a wonderful evening, isn't it?"

The two turned to look at the Colonel. Gary Hendricks extended his hand. "Yes, it's wonderful. You and your wife have done a great job putting all this together."

Colonel Mitchell smiled. "Well, truth be told, my wife and her friends did all the work. Now tell me, what are the two of you plotting?"

Tom Barnhardt motioned for the Colonel to come into their huddle. "Did you hear what that black preacher had to say this morning?"

"You mean Doctor Drummond."

"Yeah, I guess that's his name; I really haven't paid him much attention up to now. I just thought he was another one of Steele's screw ups."

"You do know who he's married to, don't you?"

Tom nodded. "She doesn't mean anything to me."

Colonel Mitchell finished his drink and signaled for a waiter to bring him another. "So what did you think of what he had to say?"

Gary Hendricks lowered his eyes to the floor. "Well, quite frankly, we didn't care much for it. He seems to think Austin is going to be returning to First Church. Frankly, Tom and I were hoping that we'd seen the last of him."

Colonel Mitchell chuckled. "I think you're in pretty good company. There are quite a number of us that feel that way."

Tom studied the Colonel's face. "Tell me, how do you feel about First Church School?"

"Quite frankly, I think it's a drain on the parish. I didn't send my children to that school. I've been on the vestry and voted against budgets that went to underwrite that school. It just didn't seem right to me to take money that was put in the offering plate for the Lord's work and then use it to provide a private education for a bunch of privileged kids."

Gary and Tom shot knowing looks at each other. "So you wouldn't be opposed to having the school separated from the parish."

"Absolutely not! It's time the Presbyterians and Baptists carried the load. They don't appreciate what this parish has done for that school, so I say let them have it. After all, ninety percent of the students aren't even members of First Church. As I've said on numerous occasions, I don't understand why my charitable contribution to the parish should be used to provide a private school education for children chauffeured around in a Mercedes."

"We'd still call it First Church School." Gary tried to reassure the Colonel.

"You can call it whatever you want. Just don't take the money for it out of the offering plates I pass every Sunday."

"Here's the problem. We know that as long as Steele Austin is rector he'll never agree to it. We were also told that Rufus Petersen wouldn't give his consent as the Bishop either."

Colonel Mitchell smiled. "Sounds to me like your problem is solved. Austin's out of the picture and so is the bishop, at least for a while."

"That's why we need to act fast. Would you be willing to help us?"

"Seems to me all you have to do is get the majority of the vestry to vote to do it while we are without a rector and a bishop."

Gary and Tom smiled broadly. "We have a majority vote."

"What are you boys talking about?" Howard Dexter interrupted the trio.

They all grinned and shook hands with Howard. "Well, Howard, I would think this might interest you. These two fellows seem to think they have the votes on the vestry to separate the school from the parish. They want to do it while we're without a rector and a bishop to stop them."

Howard shook his head. "I'm opposed to it. The school funds and the parish funds are in my bank. They operate under that same non-profit tax number. I just don't think it's a good idea to separate them at all."

Tom Barnhardt studied Howard Dexter for several minutes as Gary and the Colonel tried to convince Howard on the merits of a separation.

Then Tom interrupted them. "Howard, what if I could guarantee you that for as long as your bank exists, the new independent school will keep all funds with you and no other. Mind you, once the school is separated, the donations from the community and corporations will most likely increase ten times over what they are now."

Howard Dexter did some quick math in his head. "Will you give that to me in writing?"

"Done."

Howard extended his hand to Tom and Gary. "Gentlemen, you now have my support as long as you retain the name of the school and it remains an Episcopal school."

Gary smiled, "Howard, I won't have it any other way."

Colonel Mitchell nodded his agreement. "Boys, you'd better get it done before Austin rides back into town."

"Well, there's quite a few of us that hope he decides not to return." Howard echoed in a voice that was just above a whisper.

Colonel Mitchell shot him a puzzled look. "Howard, I thought that you and your wife had joined the Steele Austin fan club."

Howard shook his head. "We've tried. We've really tried. There was a time when we were even becoming fond of the boy."

"What changed your mind?"

"Oh, it wasn't any one thing in particular. It's just a combination of a lot of small things over the past couple of years. I've just concluded that his leadership style is not compatible with the people in our congregation."

Colonel Mitchell pushed him. "Like what?"

"You've seen it as well as I have. I mean, the man makes decisions about finances that some of us think are really the prerogative of the vestry. He doesn't even consult with us or at least with the ones of us that matter. Some of us have tried to help him but he won't let us."

Gary was fascinated. "Did anyone try to talk to him about being more open to sound advice?"

"Gentlemen, you all know as well as I do that Steele Austin simply won't accept counsel from anyone. You can't talk to the man. He just doesn't listen. I've tried to talk to him. He doesn't care what I think. He's not interested in anything I have to say to him. He's determined to do it his way. He's just so unreasonable."

"So what is your hunch? Do you think he'll be back?"

Howard wrinkled his brow, looked down at the floor and grimaced. "Like I said, the man simply won't listen. He's got to be one of the most stubborn people I've ever met. I fear he'll be back and we'll all have to suffer his arrogance once again."

"Ugh!" Tom Barnhardt moaned. "Let's just hope and pray that doesn't happen."

chapter 12

Myrtle Beach, South Carolina is sixty miles of wide, sandy beaches. It's named after the wax myrtle bushes that grow so abundantly along the coastline. Myrtle Beach is a combination of Coney Island and Branson, Missouri. There literally is something for everyone. The area is resplendent with beautiful golf courses. There are water parks and amusement parks. Dining choices range from cheap eateries to fancy dining. Topless clubs and concert venues offer nighttime entertainment. And then there's the beach and the multitude of activities it offers. Myrtle Beach can be noisy, crowded, hot and humid. But none of those things keep the tourists away.

Twenty-five miles south of Myrtle Beach and just seventy miles north of Charleston rests a little coastal resort first discovered by the rice farmers in the 1700's. These men wanted to move their families away from the rivers and marshes of the rice plantations in the summer. While the causes of malaria were unknown at the time, they knew that their loved one's health would be better served at the ocean than by the mosquito-infested rivers.

Pawleys Island is intentionally devoid of the many attractions that bring the t-shirt crowd to Myrtle Beach year after year. The unofficial and unapologetic motto of the small community is *arrogantly shabby*. There is a laid back lifestyle that encourages barefoot living. Fishing and crabbing in the multiple creeks pass the summer days away. Rope hammocks are an earmark of the island and can be purchased in one of the few shopping villages. Then there are the stories of ghosts roaming the island. The elders love to repeat the epic sightings of gray figures.

Their young listeners never tire of hearing them. Pawleys Island, South Carolina would be the home to Steele Austin and his family for the next month. Bishop Powers and his family would occupy the house on the beach next to theirs.

"First thing we've got to do is fatten you up." Bishop Powers was sitting across from Steele at the Crab Basket, one of the favorite places for the full time residents of Pawleys.

"I just don't have much of an appetite. Randi tries to get me to eat, but I'm simply not hungry."

Steele looked around the little one room shack that was the restaurant. It was basically a clapboard structure in desperate need of paint. The linoleum on the floor was worn and cracked. The tablecloths were plastic with faded flowers. There was no air conditioning, just a couple of rotating fans blowing. Thankfully the screened windows liberally placed around the building were all open. "How did you ever find this place?"

"It's not in the guidebooks. One of the locals told me about it."

A black woman approached them. In a deep, throaty voice with a smooth southern accent she asked, "What would you gentlemen like?"

The bishop nodded for Steele to order first. Do you have a menu?"

The woman chuckled. "A menu? No, we ain't got no menu. You just tell me what you want. If we got it and William T wants to cook it, I'll bring it to you. If not, you'll have to order something else."

Steele shrugged and looked at the bishop. "Do you have a salad?"

"I suppose we could put one together but you too skinny to be eating rabbit food."

Bishop Powers agreed. "Yes, he is. How about you bring him something that will put some meat on his bones. I'll have whatever you bring him. "

The woman studied Steele. "Hmm, I thinks I know just what you needs." She then yelled at the cook that was standing at the open window separating the tiny kitchen from the restaurant. "William T, we got a skinny one over here that we need to feed. Do me up a basket of hush puppies. Then make him a big platter of shrimp and grits. That'll be his first course, then we'll see where we go from there." William

T nodded and immediately went to work. "I'll bring the both of you a nice glass of cold sweet tea."

Bishop Powers turned his gaze on Steele. "From what you've told me so far, you're having some real doubts about your priesthood."

"I'm beginning to think I made a mistake. Maybe I should be doing something else."

"Fair enough. You've had quite a ride in Falls City. You've told me what you don't like about your ministry there. Now, I want you to tell me some of the things that you've done at First Church that you think really helped people."

"Like what?"

"I want you to tell me what you've done there that brings you the greatest satisfaction."

"There are several things that we did, but there was tremendous controversy around each of them."

"And they were?"

"I guess I could take them in order. We started a soup kitchen. We led a community wide service for people living with HIV and AIDS. I'm told it was the first time that the black preachers had ever been invited to do anything at First Church." Steele paused for a minute. "Then we started a free medical clinic and a halfway house for home-less, gay teenagers."

"These are all things that the congregation wanted you to do?"

Steele frowned. "No, most all the leaders of the congregation opposed them."

"The Bishop nodded. "So what did you do that the leaders asked you to do?"

"Well, they told me they wanted their parish to grow."

"And has it grown?"

"Oh my gosh, Bishop. We've had to add services. Our member-ship rolls have grown. We even get a lot of folks in church on Sunday that aren't members. Most Sundays the services are packed."

Bishop Powers grinned. "That's good. Now, my experience is that when vestries and search committees say they are looking for a rector to grow their parish, they have a particular kind of growth in mind."

"Oh?"

"Yes, they want more members that look just like the ones they currently have. So I guess those are the kind of people you attracted to the parish?"

Steele blushed. "No, that's not possible. Everyone that was on the social registry was already a member. No, in order to grow the church I had to reach out to the broader community."

The bishop nodded knowingly. "And worship. You said you had added services. Did you change the liturgy?"

"I had to. The worship services were dead when I got there. They needed to be brought to life. I mean, now we have moving processions, more contemporary music and…" Excitement rose in Steele's voice. "The congregation even applauds when something happens they like."

"Sounds good. I guess that was also what the leaders wanted you to do. They asked you to liven up their worship services when they called you."

Steele was beginning to feel defensive. "Not directly. They did say they wanted me to grow the parish. I couldn't grow the parish if the worship services were boring. You know that."

"I know it, but did they?"

"What are you saying, Bishop?" Steele was really beginning to get flustered.

"Calm down. I'm on your side. I just need you to see it from their side."

Steele sat back in his chair. He picked at one of the hushpuppies the waitress brought them. He silently stirred the shrimp and grits.

Bishop Powers allowed the silence between the two of them while he ate his lunch.

Steele pushed his still full plate away from him. "Okay, I hear what you're saying. I was doing what Jesus would have done in every one of those situations. I am proud of everything that I did and I would do it all again."

"That's not the question, Steele."

Steele was really feeling defensive. "Then just what is the question?"

Bishop Powers smiled at him. "Steele, if the next month is going to be a time of discernment and growth, then you must not become defensive. You are one of my boys. I love you and I am proud of you. Personally, I think that God does have His hand on you and He wants you to be one of His priests." The bishop watched Steele absorb his words. "But Steele, what I think doesn't matter. It's what you think that is the deciding factor."

"I don't know what I think."

"I know that. That is the very reason that I need to ask you some hard questions over the next thirty days. Only you can answer them. My hope is that when I'm finished, you will be closer to knowing just how you feel about being a priest."

Steele closed his eyes.

"Are you praying?"

"No, I can't even do that anymore."

"Okay. That's enough for one day. I want you to just think about the questions I've asked you today and your answers. Then let's get together again."

Steele nodded.

"Now, Steele, you didn't eat your lunch, so you've got to be punished."

"Huh?"

"You heard me." The bishop signaled for the waitress. "Do you have any peach cobbler made with fresh South Carolina peaches?"

"William T just pulled it out of the stove. It's piping hot."

"I thought that was what I smelled. Now bring us each a bowl with a big helping of vanilla ice cream on it."

"Yes suh."

"One more thing. You got a razor strap back there?"

The woman gave the bishop a confused look. "I'll have to ask William T."

"Well, if you've got one bring it to me because I'm going to use it on this boy here if he doesn't eat every bite of your peach cobbler."

The waitress nodded and smiled. She pointed her finger at Steele, "And I'sa get William T to hold you down while your daddy here lashes you." Her chuckles filled the room as she walked away from their table toward the serving window.

Steele tried to smile, but he was afraid the bishop just might be serious. When she brought him the hot peach cobbler smothered in vanilla ice cream, Steele ate every bite.

chapter 13

MRS. GORDON SMYTHE is the unchallenged Alpha Dog of the women of First Church. Mary Alice Smythe's prestige in Falls City had nothing to do with money or her address. Deference was given to her because of the superior blood pulsating through her veins and that of her husband. Her first lieutenant for as long as anyone could remember had been Mrs. Howard Dexter. The only other person in the parish that even dared to go up against Mary Alice Smythe was Almeda Alexander Drummond. The fact that Almeda's dead husband's ancestral tree trumped both hers and that of her husband gave her a bit of an edge. Now that Almeda's second husband was the acting rector of First Church, Almeda planned on using that edge to her advantage. Mary Alice Smythe didn't like it one bit, but she would have to temporarily defer to Almeda's superior position.

Almeda had summoned Mrs. Smythe and Mrs. Dexter to a meeting at her expansive home on exclusive River Street. Neither of the ladies could afford a home in that neighborhood. Mind you, they each had beautiful homes but their husbands had simply not been the generous providers that Almeda's first husband, Chadsworth, had been. Of course, Chadsworth did have a leg up since the family money he inherited would have been more than enough to provide for a luxurious lifestyle for several lifetimes.

Mrs. Dexter's house was perhaps the most meager of the three. The house itself was nicely situated on an upscale street just three blocks over from River Street. Her husband, however, had no interest in improvements or doing anything to the house that he considered frivolous. The wallpaper had not been changed in over twenty years and was beginning to show age. The area rugs on the wood floors were even older and becoming threadbare. Mrs. Dexter explained them as antiques she had inherited from her grandmother and that she simply couldn't bring herself to part with them. She had repeatedly asked Howard to take down the wall between the kitchen and the breakfast area in order to make it one large room. He had refused, saying he did not want to eat in the kitchen where the *Help* was preparing his breakfast. He would not give her money for new dishes, appliances or to plant flowers in the beds out front. She was left to use her dishes and appliances until they were all broken or completely beyond repair before he would allow her to go to the discount house to buy more. As for flowers in the front of her house, she had learned to ask her friends for cuttings from their beautiful gardens that she could transplant to her own.

Almeda had prepared coffee and her special sticky buns. The buns were woven with cinnamon, butter and brown sugar on the inside and were dripping with vanilla frosting on the outside. The pecans were lightly sprinkled over the top. Almeda preferred to serve them hot. They had to be eaten with a fork. She had her houseboy bring them to the small poolside table on a silver tray. She had also instructed him to use her white napkins with the red trim that had tiny bows on the bottom. She wanted him to use her Royal Doulton dessert plates, cups and saucers. He was to bring the coffee in the new silver service that she had just purchased in Atlanta. She had ordered an arrangement of tulips of appropriate size to be placed at the center of the table. Even though tulips were out of season, they remained one of her favorite flowers. She thought they would add a pleasant touch to the table.

Martha Dexter's eyes widened when Almeda's houseboy brought out the sticky buns. "Oh my goodness, Almeda, they smell absolutely wonderful!"

Almeda gave her a prideful smile. "I know that they are horribly fattening, but I think we can all afford to be just a little sinful this morning."

Martha Dexter immediately reached for the largest bun on the platter and hurriedly brought it to her mouth.

Mary Alice Smythe shot her a disapproving look. "Martha, I believe Almeda has provided us with these lovely plates and beautiful forks to eat the buns with."

Martha continued to chew while the white frosting covered her lips and oozed out of the sides of her mouth. She pushed the oversized bite of bun into her mouth with her fingers. Now they too were covered with frosting. She placed the remainder of the bun on the plate in front of her. Mary Alice picked up her napkin and looked straight into Martha's eyes. She wiped her own clean mouth with the napkin, motioning Martha do the same with her frost covered one.

Almeda watched the entire mime act with some amusement. "Ladies, I asked you to have coffee with me this morning so that we could discuss some of the changes that we need to make at our church in Steele's absence."

Mary Alice had just taken a sip of her coffee. She replaced the cup on the saucer. "Almeda, I heard Horace say in his sermon that there would be no changes while Misturh Austin's away."

Almeda forced a smile. "Ladies, we all have husbands and we all know that they don't always know what is best. The changes I am proposing are subtle and will virtually go unnoticed by my sweet man."

Martha swallowed the last bite of her sticky bun and reached for another. With her mouth still full she asked, "Almeda, what did you have in mind?" She sprayed bits of the sticky bun onto the table.

"Did you all notice that woman wearing a pantsuit in church last Sunday?"

Mary Alice frowned. "I thought that was absolutely dreadful."

Almeda was pleased to get instant agreement. "Well, I gave her one of my sternest looks. I don't believe she'll come dressed like a deck hand on a cargo ship again."

"Good for you." Martha Dexter reached for a third bun to put on her plate next to her half-eaten second one. "These are so good, Almeda."

"It would be nice if Almeda had one or two left for her husband to enjoy when he gets home." Mary Alice gave Martha a disapproving look. Martha continued to eat.

"Well, I think we need to nip all this in the bud before it even starts. I was going to put a notice in the Sunday worship leaflet instructing women to wear dresses to church. I also want men to wear coats and ties. I fear my husband will just have it removed before it even goes to print."

"So what do you suggest?" Mary Alice looked puzzled.

"I think that we should set the example. We can do it by having the altar guild participate. I've composed a letter to be mailed to all the members. The letter instructs that the members of the altar guild are to wear a head covering to church. All of us are to wear dresses or skirts that are at least knee length. It further instructs that all the men, including male children over the age of two years, are to wear coats and ties."

"Are bow ties acceptable on the children?" Martha asked with a mouth full of sticky bun.

Almeda smiled. "Absolutely. Don't you think that little boys in bow ties are so cute anyway?"

They all cooed their agreement. "By setting the example, we can obviously set the standard of dress for our church, and others will fall into place."

Martha was finishing off her third roll and started to reach for another. Mary Alice shook her head and gave her the most disapproving look of the morning. Martha withdrew her hand. "What if someone doesn't conform?"

"Then that's when we have to take direct action." Almeda sat up straight in her chair. "If someone fails to meet our standard, then one or more of us simply must speak to them. I am certainly prepared to do so. We must encourage the other members of the altar guild to be just as bold."

"I have no hesitation about speaking to the ladies on this issue, but I think that the men should monitor each other." Mary Alice said reluctantly.

"You'll be pleased to know that I have already spoken to Colonel Mitchell on this subject. It's his suggestion that we have some dark blue jackets in various sizes hanging in the usher's closet at the back of the church. They could also have some maroon clip-on ties there. If a man should arrive at the church without a jacket and tie, the ushers would simply provide one for him."

"Well, that's exactly what they do at the country club and in some of the finer restaurants." Martha Dexter quickly grabbed another bun and put it on her plate while Mary Alice wasn't looking.

"So we are all in agreement."

The two women nodded.

"That's just wonderful. I have the letter to the altar guild here. I think we all three should sign it. I will have my personal secretary copy it and send them out when she comes in this afternoon. Colonel Mitchell did have one more thought I'd like to discuss with you. He reported that on a recent trip to New York City he attended one of those posh parishes. I've forgotten which one. He said that the ushers were all wearing morning coats. He thought they looked very distinguished. It certainly added an air of formality."

Martha was staring at the remaining sticky buns. "Do you mean the formal coats that I often see at noonday weddings?"

Almeda smiled. "Exactly. What do think?"

Mary Alice grimaced. "I'll need to think about that. I am in total agreement that men should wear jackets and ties. I just need to consider further the idea of formal attire for the ushers."

"Well, we can take that up for consideration at a later date." Almeda offered reluctantly.

After they had all signed the letter to the altar guild, Almeda began to dismiss her guests. "I want to thank you for coming. I know there will be some other necessary changes we need to make and I just know I can count on your cooperation."

Mary Alice, being more savvy socially than Martha, immediately stood. "I hope you'll excuse me but I have another appointment that I simply must get to." She looked down at Martha, who was midway through her fourth bun. "Martha, I believe you rode with me. I hate to rush you but I need to go."

Martha stared at the half eaten bun on her plate. "Almeda, these sticky buns are just delicious. I wish my Howard could have enjoyed them."

Mary Alice gave Almeda an apologetic look.

"And so he should." Almeda smiled and rang the silver bell that had been sitting on the table. Her houseboy immediately responded. A very happy Martha Dexter carried the remaining sticky buns home in a plastic container that Almeda insisted she not return. Mrs. Gordon Smythe, on the other hand, was completely humiliated.

chapter 14

Bishop Elect Sean Evans had not been able to sleep or eat the past four days. His entire system was in turmoil. The one thing that he could do that seemed to help was to put on his running shoes and run. When he grew too tired to run, he'd walk. He was going out several times each day now to do one or the other. He simply could not calm the anxiety that was now his constant companion. He didn't know what was going to happen next. Not only could he be unemployed with no place to live, but he could face a humiliation that would become public knowledge. It was just the kind of thing that the secular press as well as the religious press could thrive on. He could see the headlines now. *Bishop Elect Sean Evans disqualified for sexual misconduct.* He wanted to vomit but there was nothing in his stomach to dislodge.

If his accuser turned out to be a woman, Sean had made up his mind that he'd just risk it. He'd tell John North the truth about himself. Deep down Sean knew that his accuser would be a man. He'd only had sex with men. Why would any woman accuse him since he'd shown little or no sexual interest in any female? Sean had racked his memory for every sexual encounter he'd had since he started having sex with other men. Jim Vernon had been his most constant sexual relationship the past few years, but he was not the only one. Sean had been ever so careful not to knowingly hook up with any member of the congregations in the diocese where he worked. There were two other relatively long-term relationships he'd had but they were both with other members of the clergy. One was with a married but closeted gay bishop. He was certain that he'd not want to make any accusations against Sean since it would require him to out himself.

There was the relationship that he had with the priest he met at General Convention. They ran into each other in the bar. That priest did not try to hide the fact that he was gay. He had a rainbow ribbon pinned to his nametag. He was a member of several gay organizations fighting for equality in the nation and in the Church. They'd had a passionate two-week romance that did not end well. The priest wanted them to continue to see each other as often as they could. Sean had begun tiring of him a few days before the convention was to end. He was quite frankly happy that several hundred miles separated them. At first he took his phone calls but was abrupt with him on the telephone. Finally he'd just told him that he didn't see their relationship going anywhere and there was no need for them to continue to stay in touch. Sean thought that perhaps he could have filed the accusation with the Presiding Bishop's office. He was trying to get even with Sean for breaking off their relationship.

Most of Sean's other relationships had been anonymous. He really didn't like the bar scene, but occasionally when he just needed to feel the touch of a man he'd go to the bars and pick up some guy. But he never did it in Mobile where he lived and worked. He only frequented gay bars when he was in another city. Sean tried to remember their names. He couldn't even remember most of their faces and very few of their names came forward. But then again, he didn't use his real name. He was always Michael. Most of them probably didn't use their real names either. He was certain that he'd never told any of them that he was a priest.

Normally trying to remember the names and faces of his past conquests would get Sean excited. It was a pastime he exercised on numerous occasions. On the nights he couldn't sleep and he was in need of a fantasy he would try to recall one of his past experiences. Often just remembering the person and how they felt would be enough to arouse him. Then there were the times that he'd be out running on the beach. Often he needed a distraction from the pain he was feeling in his legs and lungs. Reliving a night of anonymous sex that had been particularly passionate was a great diversion.

A new wave of panic rose up in Sean and brought him back to his current dilemma. Crap! His picture had been in every newspaper in the State of Georgia. It had been on most of the local television stations. It was all over the Internet. One of those guys could have seen his photo and decided to make the accusation. They might be hoping to blackmail him or maybe they'd thought he didn't treat them just right so they wanted to get even. Then again, maybe they just wanted to claim their moment in the sun. To unseat a bishop elect could surely get them some interviews with the media. It might even get them a book deal.

The flight from Mobile had been excruciating. He could not read the book he'd brought with him. He couldn't concentrate. The flight wasn't long enough for there to be a movie to distract him. The fat man sitting next to him had fallen asleep soon after take off. Sean was thankful for that because he was in no mood for small talk. Sean ordered two scotch whiskeys to drink and drank both of them, hoping they would help calm his nerves. He rehearsed his defense against the charges one more time. If his accuser was a woman he would simply out himself to Bishop North. It was a big risk, but he would argue that he was celibate and had been since his ordination. He knew for a fact that no woman would ever be able to place him in a compromising situation.

If his accuser was a man, his defense would be more difficult. First he'd have to try to remember just who the man was and if in fact he'd ever had sex with him. Sean needed to know the circumstances in order to assign a motive to his accuser. That would be his strongest defense in case some little queen was attempting to get even with him for something. He would simply have to discredit his accuser and expose his motives. Hopefully that would work. If needed, he could go one step further and simply admit that was his one and only slip but that he'd been celibate since. If by chance the accusation was supposed to have happened years ago, he could argue that it occurred before he was even ordained and that he'd been celibate since.

The offices of pastoral care are housed in the offices of the National Episcopal Church in New York City. Sean sat in the waiting room outside Bishop North's office. He could not hold still. He stood and paced the floor waiting for John North to invite him into his office. Sean sat down on the sofa. He crossed his legs but could not hold his fingers or his foot still. His legs actually ached with anxiety. He thumped his fingers on the arm of the sofa. Soon the door opened and John North walked toward Sean and extended his hand. "Sean. John North. I remember meeting you now. Come on in. How was your flight?"

Sean's anxiety was now overwhelmed by anger. Once they were in Bishop North's office and the door was closed, Sean exploded. "John, this entire thing is bullshit. One week ago I was a very happy man. I was the bishop elect of the Diocese of Savannah. Now I don't know what I am. My entire world has been turned upside down by some outrageous accusation. This entire thing is so bizarre. I feel like I'm in some sort of cheap reality show for late night television. The first thing I want to know is just who this lawyer is and what's my accuser's name."

"Sit down, Sean. Let's talk a bit."

"Hell no!" Sean raised his voice. "I don't want to chat! I want to see the letter. Let's get right to it."

John North flinched. "Okay, if that's the way you want to handle it."

"Show me the bullshit letter."

John North opened a manila folder with the word *CONFIDENTIAL* emblazed in red on it. He handed Sean a letter with an envelope stapled to it. Sean could see that there were other papers in the file. He quickly scanned the letter looking for the names of the attorney and his accuser. He'd never heard of the attorney. He was quite sure of that. Her office was in Bay City, which is a middle class suburb of Mobile. Then he saw the name of his accuser. He breathed a quick sigh of relief.

❧

chapter 15

VIRGINIA MUDD WAS sitting at a window table of the Main Street Café in downtown Falls City. It was her favorite table. She could sit with her back to the rest of the patrons in the café. At the same time she could watch the passersby on the sidewalk outside the restaurant. It took her awhile to get used to eating in restaurants alone, but now she'd found her comfort level. Virginia always brought a book or magazine with her so that she could lose herself in the pages while she waited on her meal to be served. If the café was devoid of patrons, she was comfortable lingering with her book and a cup of coffee. Today she was having one of her favorite sandwiches. It was a grilled pimento cheese on white bread. They served it with her choice of two side vegetables. On this day she had ordered sweet potato fries and carrot salad with raisins. Since the lunch crowd had left she was the only remaining patron. Virginia watched the various business people walking past her to their respective offices. There were several shoppers moving systematically in and out of the stores within her view. She recognized several people that at one time she would have tried to engage in conversation. Since her divorce from Henry, each of the ones that she saw had made it clear that they no longer wanted anything to do with her. They were *southern polite* but cold. She knew the drill all too well. She used to be an expert. It was her most graceful tool around people that she did not consider her equal or those that had fallen from societal grace.

Virginia hated it that her several indiscretions had become public knowledge. There was that video that one of her lovers had made without her knowledge. Her friend Alicia had told her that the video was on the social circuit and had been seen by most everyone in Falls City. In addition to that, he'd sold it to a porn website and it was on the Internet. Virginia felt her pimento sandwich coming back on her. She swallowed hard to keep it down. Then there was that detective that Henry had hired. Virginia and Henry had been such a public couple in Falls City; some of the people in the detective's office just couldn't resist such juicy gossip. Soon the truth of her secret life was expanded on and spread through the streets of the city. Now when she saw one of the people from her former life, they would try to avoid her or she would try to avoid them. When that wasn't possible, they would all resort to the polite but cold game they'd been trained in as children.

Virginia looked at her watch. She just had enough time to get to her afternoon support group. She started to stand when her heart skipped a beat. Directly across the street coming out Evelyn's Teen Shop were her two daughters and a very attractive blonde woman. Virginia wrinkled her brow as she tried to identify the woman. She'd never seen her before, or had she? She looked like the woman that had worked in Henry's office.

Virginia felt emptiness in the pit of her stomach. She studied the woman. She thought her to be so much more beautiful than she was. She just knew that the woman with her girls must be Henry's girlfriend. At the very least she was someone that he was sleeping with. Everyone in town would be talking about how much prettier she was than Virginia. She guessed her to be at least ten years younger, maybe more. The town gossips would all snicker and say that Henry had traded up. She felt so hollow.

Her daughters were carrying shopping bags. They were all smiling and laughing. Everyone looked so happy. The woman brushed the hair of her youngest daughter with her hand. Her daughter then threw her arms around the woman's waist and hugged her. Then her other daughter did the same. Right there on the sidewalk her daughters were having a group hug with a woman she knew very little about. Then the three of them joined hands and moved down the street out of Virginia's sight.

Virginia fell back in her chair. Large tears streamed down her face. She hurt. Her heart hurt. That should be her. She should be taking her daughters shopping. She should be the one hugging them and putting those big smiles on their faces. She was their mother. They belonged to her. She brought them into this world. It wasn't fair. Virginia felt so lonely. She was empty.

"You all right, lady?"

Virginia looked up and wiped her eyes. Through the blur she could see that it was a waiter. She nodded.

"You look like a woman with a problem. A beautiful woman like you shouldn't have any problems. That's just not right." He smiled.

Virginia wiped her face again and tried to compose herself. She studied his face. He was sort of handsome. He had straight white teeth and blue eyes. His hair was a bit unruly, but otherwise the white t-shirt and blue jeans he was wearing revealed a slim, athletic body. He was quite a bit younger. She wasn't even sure if he was legal, but he'd called her *beautiful*. That felt so good.

"Mind if I sit down?"

Virginia smiled and gave him her best single's bar stare. The man sat down. They talked for well over an hour. Virginia rubbed the man's leg with her foot underneath the table. She put her hand on his leg several times, leaving no doubt of her intentions. "What time do you get off work?"

"I'm off now."

"You want to come over to my house? I mean, I don't have any alcohol to drink but I have plenty of coffee or sweet tea." Once again she looked deep into his eyes so that he could not mistake her intentions.

"Sure, why not? My name's Craig."

"And I'm Virginia." She wrote her address and telephone number on Craig's hand. She squeezed it with both of hers. "See you soon, Craig." She closed the deal by offering him her most seductive smile.

Virginia quickly showered when she got home. She applied fresh makeup and put a silk bathrobe over her naked body. Virginia knew what she needed and Craig was going to provide it. Just then she heard a knock at the door.

"Well, I see you're dressed for a party." Craig's breath smelled of liquor. He pushed past her, brushing his body against hers, leaving little to either of their imaginations. "I have to admit that I didn't expect this. I figured you for one of them rich socialite wives."

"I used to be." Virginia whimpered.

The man turned and leered at her. "Used to be. My guess is that your husband caught you cheating on him and threw your ass out." He removed a pint bottle of bourbon from his rear jeans pocket and took a swallow from it. He handed the bottle to Virginia. "Here, you need this more than I do."

Virginia shook her head. "No, I don't drink."

"Well, if I were you I'd sure as hell start. Here, take a drink." He held the bottle underneath her nose. The odor was so familiar to her. It was an old friend. Virginia took the bottle and quickly gulped several swallows.

The man grabbed the bottle from her. "Whoa there. Save some for me. For a non-drinker it appears to me you really know how to hold your liquor." Then Craig put his arms around Virginia and kissed her. He forced her mouth open with his tongue and forced it into her throat.

Virginia pulled away from him. He smelled awful. He smelled of dead fish or worse. Virginia felt herself gag.

"Hey, what the hell is that all about?"

"Maybe this is not such a good idea. Craig, I don't think this is going to work for me."

"Like hell." He yelled. "You invite me over here and get me all hot and bothered and then play hard to get. To hell with that! This is going to happen and it's going to happen right now." He grabbed for her. She pushed against him but he was too strong for her. He ripped her sheer silk bathrobe off her until she stood naked before him. "Oh, I'm going to enjoy this. I've never had me a society woman, even if she does live in a mill village now."

Virginia continued to struggle against him. "Leave me alone. Get out of my house!" She yelled. His smell was nauseating.

Craig slapped Virginia across her cheek and ear. Her ear and face stung. She grabbed her ear and felt moisture. She looked at her hand. It had blood on it. "Now lay down, bitch. We're going to do this right here on the floor and you're going to enjoy it."

Virginia reached around him and pulled the liquor bottle from his back pocket. She swung it at his head with all her strength. The bottle broke open on his temple as he staggered back from her. He looked at her stunned. She held the broken bottle in front of her, wielding the only weapon she had. "Now you get out of my house and you get out now or I'm going to call the police."

Craig continued to mop the blood from his face with the bottom of his t-shirt. He staggered toward the door. He waved his hand at her dismissively. "Oh, to hell with it. You probably aren't any good anyway. It wouldn't be worth it."

Virginia slammed the door behind him and double locked it. She collapsed to the floor and buried her face in her knees. Great sobs shook her body as she rocked back and forth. "I need help. I need help. Oh God, help me."

⚜

chapter 16

THE VESTRY OF First Church had become decidedly less supportive of Steele Austin. At the last annual meeting the forces intent on separating the school from the parish had successfully elected Elmer Idle as senior warden and Gary Hendricks as junior warden. Those gathered then insured the success of their venture by electing four new vestry members that were also loyal to their endeavor. Now things had changed slightly. Stone Clemons and Chief Sparks were determined to rebalance the scales. Both men were strong supporters of the rector and both were strongly opposed to the manipulating work that they knew for a fact Tom Barnhardt and Gary Hendricks were doing.

In the absence of the rector and the senior warden, Gary Hendricks, as junior warden, called the meeting to order. He asked Doctor Drummond to lead the vestry in prayer. Following the prayer he called for approval of the minutes of the last meeting. The financial statement was presented next. It showed that pledge and plate collections were well ahead of budget projections. The treasurer had directed that the excess operating funds be transferred to the operating reserve.

Gary pontificated. "As the junior warden I'd like to remind you that at the last meeting of the vestry, we presented a resolution to form a committee to begin the process of having the school become an independent corporation separate from the parish. The rector's abrupt departure from that meeting and subsequently his absence from the parish required that we table that resolution. I see no reason why we should not bring it forward for a vote at this meeting."

Gary's words were followed by nods of agreement.

Stone Clemons rose to his feet. "Gentlemen, I can think of several reasons that we cannot bring such a resolution to the table for a vote."

"Like what?" Gary Hendricks clearly was irritated with Stone.

"Well, just look around this room. You are not just talking about a change in governance; you are talking about giving away real estate holdings that are owned by the corporate entities known as First Church and the Diocese of Savannah."

"That's exactly what we intend to do." Gary rebuffed Stone.

"Sir, we have no senior warden at the current time. We've all received notice that Elmer Idle is no longer a member of this congregation. Our rector is absent and on sabbatical. Further, we are currently without a sitting bishop."

"So this vestry is the fiduciary of the parish and school. We are free to make any decision that we want to make."

A broad smile crossed Stone's face. "No sir, we are not. The Constitution and Canons of the Episcopal Church clearly state that no property shall be sold or transferred without the consent of the bishop of the diocese and the standing committee."

"Where does it say that?" Gary clearly could not hide his anger.

"I've made copies for each of you." Stone began passing the copies around the table.

"Now I've also made copies of the diocesan canons and by-laws of the parish that clearly state that the rector of the parish is in charge of all educational endeavors conducted by the parish, including parochial day schools. You will also notice that in the absence of the rector, the bishop of the diocese becomes the rector with all the same authority and responsibility."

"Are you trying to tell me that we won't be able to bring this resolution to a vote until Steele Austin returns?"

Stone nodded. "In part that's exactly what I am telling you. Under the procedures section of the diocesan canons you'll notice that petitions to sell or transfer property, once approved by the vestry, must be personally presented to the bishop and standing committee by the rector and senior warden. Sir, we have no bishop, no rector, and no senior warden. Three key players in the process are missing."

"I don't see any reason that the vestry can't approve this resolution and Doctor Drummond and I will take it to the standing committee. I can do so as the junior warden."

"Hold on there, Mister Hendricks." Horace Drummond rose to his feet. "I've already made it clear that nothing is going to change in the rector's absence. I'll have nothing to do with this resolution, especially one with such far reaching consequences."

"Then I'll just take it myself."

Stone nodded. "If you wish. I think you'll be successful getting it passed tonight by one vote if I've read the table correctly. But you need to know that I've prepared a letter for the remaining members of the vestry to sign that I will also present to the standing committee. The letter asks them to reject your request since we are without our rector and a bishop at this time."

Horace Drummond supported Stone's statement. "And you need to know that not only will I go with Mister Clemons to the Standing Committee to present that letter, but Mother Graystone and our deacon will also be there to present a united clergy support."

Gary Hendricks sat back in his chair. A look of defeat crossed his face. He threw his hands out in front of him in exasperation. "It just doesn't seem right that if this governing body votes to do something that we can't then execute that decision."

Chief Sparks chuckled. "Welcome to the Episcopal Church."

"So it would be useless to pass this resolution tonight." Gary uttered.

"I'd suggest that you hold on to it until we have a bishop and a rector back in place. Even then I'd test the water. If the vestry votes in favor but either the rector or bishop are opposed to it, your resolution is dead. "

"Then I don't guess there's anything for us to do here tonight. We might as well go home."

"Not so fast." Chief Sparks stood. "I have an amendment to the by-laws that I would like to offer under new business."

"What kind of amendment?" Gary shot back at him.

"I have copies. It is a very simple by-law change. It concerns the manner in which we elect our senior warden. I think that the entire parish is fully aware of the way our last senior warden was elected. Clearly we all understand the politics involved and the motives for electing him. Since his removal from the parish by none other than the bishop, all of this has now become crystal clear. The change to the by-laws I am proposing removes the election of the senior and junior wardens from the political arena."

"I don't like what I'm hearing." Gary's voice filled the room.

"With all due respect, sir, I'd like to continue." While Gary started studying the paper that the Chief had distributed, he continued. "Under this by-law change, the senior warden would be appointed from the elected vestry by the rector and the junior warden would be a vestry person elected by their fellow vestry members."

Several at the table nodded their agreement. Gary Hendricks shook his head. "I see nothing wrong with the way we currently elect these two offices."

Chief Sparks frowned at him. "Then, sir, you have only increased my disappointment in you. You see nothing wrong with secret meetings in the parish. You see nothing wrong with malicious telephone banks designed to slander other candidates. You see nothing wrong with getting people to come to the annual meeting who haven't been to worship in years for the sole purpose of casting a politically motivated vote. You see nothing wrong with encouraging people who are not even members of this parish to come to our meeting to do the same."

Gary hung his head. "I think you've greatly exaggerated the situation. You are trying to demonize those of us that only have the best interest of the parish at heart."

The Chief shot him a long hard look. "That notwithstanding, I am moving this change to the by-laws. I encourage the vestry members to consider it as a way to heal some of the divisions that this last election has brought to our parish family."

Before the Chief could even sit down, a second to the by-law change was offered by one of the new vestry.

Gary couldn't believe his ears. "You're going to second this?"

"I am. I was elected to the vestry by a group of people that knew I would vote in favor of separating the school. I still believe that's the right thing to do and when the time comes, that's exactly how I am going to vote. But gentlemen, I don't like the way I was elected. The entire process from start to finish simply was not Christian. I might as well have been at a political caucus. At least here in the church our leaders should be elected because they want to serve for the advancement of the Gospel and not because of some agenda item. They definitely should not be elected because it is believed they will keep the rector in line or worse."

Stone nodded at the young man. "Thank you for your honesty. And thank you for your witness."

"Well, I'm opposed to this by-law change and I'm going to vote against it. I see nothing wrong with the way we elect our wardens." Gary rebutted. His face was beet red with anger.

Chief Sparks gave him a long hard stare one more time. Then he sadly shook his head, "Of course you don't."

The vote was eleven to one to approve the change in the by-laws. Gary did not stay for the closing prayer. He rushed out of the building. As soon as he arrived at his house he rushed to the telephone and dialed. "Tom, you aren't going to believe what they've done now. We've got to figure out a way to put Steele Austin's fan club out of business."

chapter 17

"STEELE, I HAVE a hair and nail appointment. I need to leave now. "

"Sounds like you're getting a double dip."

"Funny man. You just don't realize how much work it is to be girl. But you do like the results, don't you?"

Steele took Randi in his arms and kissed her. "I like what I see right now. I think you are perfect just the way you are."

Randi squeezed Steele's bicep. "Then you're really going to like what you see when I get back. What are you and kids going to do?"

"I told Travis that we'd go play golf while you were getting your hair done. He's excited about that. I also promised him ice cream. Then I'm going to meet Bishop Powers on the beach. I thought maybe while we talk Travis could play in the sand. I'm hoping Amanda will be ready for a nap by then."

"Not too much ice cream, Steele."

"For me or Travis?"

"Travis can have a kiddie cup. You should have a triple dip and then follow it up with a malt."

"What are you saying?"

"I'm saying that one of the things I want to see you do on this sabbatical is put some meat back on those bones."

"You don't want me to get fat, do you?"

"I don't think that will be a problem. Just get back to your fighting weight."

"Now Randi, you do remember that I'm a lover and not a fighter."

Randi gave him a big smile and kissed him on the cheek. "Yes you are, *big boy*. You're quite the lover."

After she'd gone, Steele put Amanda and Travis in their car seats and drove them to the miniature golf course in Surfside Beach just north of Pawleys Island. Choosing a miniature golf course along the recreational coast known as Myrtle Beach is the real challenge. Finding one is not difficult at all. They litter the coastal highway. Steele mused that there must be one miniature golf course per tourist. Once he had parked his car in front of a course, he had to keep an excited Travis in his car seat until he could get Amanda in her stroller. Travis was energized. The miniature golf course had multiple features including a castle, various animals, a waterfall, and a clown. As soon as Steele handed Travis his plastic golf club and a blue golf ball, Travis started running toward the clown. "Wait, Travis. We have to start over here."

"No, daddy, I want the clown. I want to put my ball in the clown's mouth."

"Travis, come back. Come here. Let me show you something."

Travis ran back to where Steele was standing with Amanda. "Look, son. See the numbers. Each course has numbers. We have to start with the first one and then wait our turn to play. Remember, we've talked about taking turns."

"Okay, Daddy. Let's play."

Travis took multiple strokes on each hole. When he couldn't get the ball to go in with his club he'd simply pick it up and drop it in the hole. "Who won, Daddy?"

"You did. Now let's go get some ice cream."

"Amanda can't eat ice cream."

"That's fine. I brought a bottle for her."

"I want chocolate."

"Of course you do. You are your father's son."

On the beach in front of their beach house, Steele put up an umbrella and put Travis with his beach toys under it. Amanda had fallen asleep in the car and remained so. He placed her on a blanket underneath the umbrella. He figured she would sleep for another hour.

"Have you thought about the questions I asked you at lunch?" Bishop Powers lit a cigarette and sat down in a beach chair next to Steele. Together they watched Travis play and Amanda sleep.

"I have. I have to tell you they've kept me awake the last couple of nights."

"Good."

"What's good about not sleeping?"

"I've found that God can use insomnia to speak to us. Just remember to listen."

Steele nodded. "What do you want to talk about today?"

"I fear I'm going to give you some more insomnia." Bishop Powers put out his cigarette and looked at Steele. "Before we begin, I want you to know that I love you and I believe in you. One of the things I admire about you is the fact that you're willing to be honest with yourself."

Steele felt his stomach flip. "Why do I feel like my dad is just about to take me out behind the barn for a whipping?"

"That's not my intent. But there are some things I need to ask you and you need to hear your answers. It's really not even the answers that are important. It's just important that you verbalize the answers and then hear what you're saying."

"Okay. Shoot."

"What were you thinking when you hired a detective to follow your wife?" The Bishop lit another cigarette. "No, let me reword that. I know what you thought she was doing. Help me understand the factors that led you to take such a dramatic step."

Steele shrugged. "First, you need to know that Randi and I have talked this through several times and we've each resolved to make some changes."

"Before we get to those changes, start at the beginning."

"There are several things that I now realize led me to do what I did."

"Go on."

"I don't offer any of this as an excuse. I think these are the factors that led me to make the decision I did. First, I'd spent the last year pastoring one of the men in my church that discovered his wife had multiple affairs. He trusted her. He thought he had a good marriage. He just never believed that she would do anything like that. Then he discovered that she'd not only had one affair but several. She even aborted a baby that she conceived with one of her lovers."

"Did you get caught up in his story?"

"I fear I did. This was a man that had opposed my ministry. Then he asked me to be his pastor. We became very close during our counseling sessions. He's now one of my best friends."

"Did you lose your objectivity?"

"I tried not to, but my heart really went out to him. He was so wounded. His hurt did become my hurt. I suppose I was not able to maintain a clinical distance from him."

"And you transferred his experience to your own marriage. How?"

"Again, I am not making excuses, but some of the things his wife was doing Randi also was doing. Some of those red flags he simply should have seen."

"And so you thought there were red flags in Randi's behavior."

Steele nodded. "Bishop, Randi is a flirt. I've always known she is a flirt. I would probably have never asked her out if she hadn't flirted with me the first time I saw her."

"Did you ever call her a flirt?"

"There were times that her behavior made me really uncomfortable, especially at social gatherings. I'd confronted her several times but she always reassured me that I was just being silly. She'd kiss men on their lips."

"What?" Bishop Powers wrinkled his brow.

"Just what I said. She'd kiss men on their lips. Sometimes she'd do it when she was saying *hello*. Then again when we would be leaving."

"I hope you told her that made you uncomfortable."

"I did, but she said I was just being silly. She was only being friendly. Randi called them innocent little pecks. I tried to tell her that watching her do that was really humiliating for me. I'd never seen any other wife go around lip kissing men. She would tell me how much she loved me and I would drop it. I suppose I should have been more firm with her."

"I would certainly agree with that. Was your parishioner's wife a flirt?"

"She was blatant about it. But she told her husband the same thing. She said she was just being friendly."

"And when you received the pictures, what kept you from just asking Randi about them?"

Steele sat back in his chair and stared out at the ocean. The silence was uncomfortable for both of them. Steele broke the silence. "Bishop Powers, let me ask you a question. How many adulterers have you known in your ministry?"

"More than I care to remember over my thirty years in the parish."

"And how many of those adulterers owned up to what they were doing when they were first confronted by their spouse?"

"None." The Bishop lit another cigarette. He drew in the smoke and held it in his lungs, lost in thought. As he exhaled the smoke he nodded. "Okay. Point taken."

"That was another factor that led me to do what I did. I needed to know. Frankly, I figured that if Randi was having an affair and I asked her about it she'd deny it. Bishop, I needed the facts."

"And if she had been?"

"I love her. I love her with all my heart, but I saw the pain that wife's infidelity put my friend through. I can only tell you the pain and anxiety I felt just suspecting Randi. I honestly don't see how any marriage can survive it."

"You and I both know the overwhelming majority don't."

"Have you asked Randi why she didn't tell you about the encounter with the young man in the picture?"

"I did, but it was late in one of our conversations. Our initial talks all began with me taking the responsibility for the entire thing. I had to apologize several times before we could get to that point."

"And?"

Steele took a deep breath. "She did remember the encounter. She also thought it was pretty innocent and there really was no need to tell me about it."

"And you accepted that?"

"At first I did, but then I got angry. If a half naked woman had rubbed up against me and unbuttoned my swim trunks I'd feel the need to tell her about it. I would rather she hear it from me than some gossip."

"Go on."

"So I pushed her on it. She said she was operating from the principle that what I didn't know didn't hurt me."

The Bishop gave Steele a sideways look. "I certainly hope you didn't let that one stand?"

Steele nodded toward the children. Travis was asleep on the blanket under the umbrella next to his sister. "Right there are the two best reasons I know not to let that sort of thinking continue in our marriage. I asked her to not ever think that way again. Basically, that amounts to keeping secrets. You and I both know we don't keep secrets; our secrets keep us. And that one secret almost destroyed our marriage. She understood and agreed. We both agreed not to keep any secret, no matter how innocent, from each other."

"That's a lesson some couples never learn until it's too late." The Bishop put out his cigarette and stood to leave. "You're going to need to do some daddy work in just a few minutes and I need to get out of this sun."

Steele could see that both Amanda and Travis were stirring. "When do you want to meet again?

"In a couple of days. I'll call you." The bishop started to walk away and then turned back to look at Steele. "What about the flirting?"

Steele picked Amanda up and took Travis by the hand. Travis stood rubbing the sleep out of his eyes. "She's promised to stop. Or at least listen to me when certain behaviors make me uncomfortable."

Bishop Powers stood looking at Steele and his two children. "Do you have any idea the number of marriages and families that could be saved if the couples would simply learn the lessons that Randi and you have learned from this experience?"

Steele nodded. "No secrets."

"That's one."

"And the other?'

"If you're going to play on a slippery bank you just might fall in the water."

Steele wrinkled his forehead. "Huh?"

"Flirting. It's a slippery bank. Married people should not play on slippery banks."

chapter 18

"TELL US WHAT you have planned, Harlan." Elmer Idle and Ned Boone had invited Harlan McMurray to meet with them at the grill in the Falls City Country Club. They had each ordered *a nineteenth hole hamburger*.

"I thought the first thing we'd do is write some letters to the presbytery up in Savannah."

"Savannah?" Ned flinched. "Why do you have to write to Savannah? I thought each Presbyterian Church was self-governing. We don't want to get involved with any bishop types that can overrule us."

"Our local session can do pretty much whatever they want to but we have to make the regional presbytery aware of the fact that the congregation is not happy with our preacher."

Elmer Idle winked at Ned. "Now Harlan, you need to understand. We're here to help because, quite frankly, we don't care for your preacher. He doesn't impress us at all. We'd all like to make St. Andrew's our church home, but not if we're going to get involved in some long drawn out process with some office up in Savannah."

"I understand. It's different than what you all had to deal with as Episcopalians. The presbytery can't overrule us if we ask the preacher to leave. But politically, when it comes to replacing him, we need to make sure they're on our side."

Elmer sat back in his seat. "Well, that makes sense to me. Does it to you, Ned?"

"How many people do you have that are willing to write letters?" Ned asked.

"I've only personally talked to about a half dozen, but everyone I've talked to tells me they are speaking for dozens of other members."

Ned waved at the waiter. "You boys want a cup of coffee?" They both nodded and Ned indicated for the waiter to bring them each some coffee. I guess if letter writing to Savannah is necessary then you can count on both of us to write one. But frankly, I don't feel the necessary momentum in the congregation to get things started. It appears to me that your preacher is pretty popular."

"He is with his fan club but none of the people that really matter in this congregation are members of his fan club."

"The church was full last Sunday. Is the money coming in?"

"Oh, he can fill the pews and the session has plenty of money to blow on his pet projects. There is a large segment of the congregation that simply does not care for the man."

Elmer Idle smiled at Ned. "Seems like we've been here before."

Ned nodded. "Have you had any cottage meetings?"

"Yes. Every Lent we have cottage meetings as a part of our program."

"No. That's not what I mean." Ned continued. "Have you gotten the people together that think that your preacher's time has come?"

Harlan shook his head. "No. We've haven't done anything like that."

Ned frowned. "Well, what have you done?"

"Those of us that want him to go have talked among ourselves at the coffee hour after church but that's as far as we've gone. All of us have agreed to write the letters to the presbytery."

Ned thumped his fingers on the table. "Tell you what, Harlan. That simply is not going to get the job done."

"Well, what do you suggest?"

Elmer chuckled. "For the answer to that question you've come to the right place. Ned here can outline a fail proof plan for you. If you follow it you'll be in the market for a new preacher within ninety days."

"That sounds good." A big smile crossed Harlan's face. "Tell me what you think we should do."

Ned sat up tall in his chair. "First, I need to meet the people you've been talking with. When does your session meet?"

"The second Wednesday of every month."

"Are the meetings open to the congregation?"

"Sure, but no one has ever gone, so far as I know."

"That's going to change at the next meeting. We need four or five people to attend."

"For what purpose?"

Ned and Elmer started laughing. "To raise their level of anxiety. To fill them with a little paranoia, but most of all to make your preacher nervous."

"Are they going to say anything?"

"No. Their presence at the meeting will say it all, but they need to be present in ever growing numbers at every meeting until we get rid of the preacher."

"And that works?"

"It's part of the plan. Then we need to get everyone that agrees with us to start hosting some secret cottage meetings to talk about our unhappiness with the preacher. We have to get them excited about the possibility of getting rid of him."

"What if someone comes that supports him?"

"That might happen, but we just have to make sure they're shouted down if they try to speak."

"Anything else?"

"Yes, then we start putting the pressure on him."

"How do we do that?"

"Ask for an audit of any funds that he controls. Ask for an accounting of his time. Are there any staff members that don't care for him?"

"I know the bookkeeper doesn't like him. And then I think the youth minister and he have butted heads quite a few times. I don't think there's any love lost there."

"Good. Bring both of them into the loop. They can be of immense help. Let them know what we are trying to do."

"Gosh, Ned, this all sounding like it just might work."

"Oh, it'll work. Do you have anything on him?"

"Like what?"

"Oh, you know the usual; sex, drugs, booze, finances."

"No. As far as I know he's Mister Clean."

"Well, let's find out. I will personally hire a detective to do some looking around in his background. We need to get a few folks to contact members of his former congregations. We just need to find a little dirt and then exaggerate it."

Harlan looked down at the table as though he were trying to read some invisible words printed on it. "I don't know, guys. I just want him to leave. I don't know if I want to destroy his ministry, and that's exactly what we might end up doing."

Elmer put his hand on Harlan's arm. "Harlan, let's just hope it doesn't come to that. We only need to get him on the run. Then he'll leave."

"What if your detective doesn't find anything?"

Ned grinned. "Oh, he'll find something. No man is perfect. You have my personal guarantee that he will find something on your preacher that we can use against him."

Harlan nodded. "Okay. I guess we have a plan. Now we only need to start working it."

"So be it." Elmer agreed.

"Ned. Elmer. Don't you think it's a strange coincidence that out of all the people you met on your first Sunday at St. Andrew's you met me? And don't you find it interesting that you had the same reaction to the preacher that my friends and I have?"

Elmer pointed his finger first at Harlan and then at Ned. "Gentlemen, that was no coincidence. God's hand was in it all. He brought us to St. Andrew's and he led us to you, Harlan. He knew that we could help you get rid of your preacher. You can take that to the bank. It was God. And God is going to bless our work to do what needs to be done at St. Andrew's."

chapter 19

"Do you know the woman?" Bishop John North asked Sean Evans.

Sean looked up from the letter the bishop had handed him. He looked around the bishop's office. It was on the eleventh floor of the National Church Office building in New York City. Sean thought it looked so much like all the other bishop's offices he'd been in. The color purple was everywhere. On the wall hung the bishop's framed certificate of consecration with all the consecrating bishops' wax seals on it. Then there was the customary photo of the bishops laying hands on him at his ordination. The other photos were also predictable. A large photo of the bishop and all the bishops present at the Lambeth Conference held every ten years by the Archbishop of Canterbury in England. A picture of Bishop North with Desmond Tutu dominated one of the walls. Then there were pictures of him with a couple of political and Hollywood celebrities. Sean resolved not to have any of it in his office if he could just get through this mess.

"Canon Evans, do you know the woman?"

"I don't know the attorney. I've never heard of her."

"And the woman making the accusation?"

Sean frowned. He strained to bring the woman into his memory bank. "I have to confess that the name sounds familiar but I can't place her."

Bishop North looked surprised. He studied Sean's face. He analyzed his body language. "You realize that you must be absolutely honest with me. If I don't feel like you're being honest with me, I will have no choice but to recommend that your election be declared null and void."

Sean looked him directly in the eye. "I have no intention but to be one thousand percent honest with you."

Bishop North's facial expression became very stern. "Sean, I need to know if you know this woman. She has made a very serious accusation against you."

Again Sean searched his memory. He knew the name but he just couldn't put it into context. "I'm telling you that the name sounds familiar, but I just can't call up a face or even remember meeting her."

The bishop leaned back in his chair. Clearly he was getting exasperated with Sean. He then sorted through the papers in the file on his desk. "Okay, maybe this will help. The woman is a member of Holy Cross Parish in Darwood, Alabama."

Sean closed his eyes. The picture of Holy Cross Parish came into view. "That parish is in our diocese. I've been there several times in my capacity as deployment officer for the diocese. I met with the vestry and search committee while they were looking for a rector."

"So you know the woman?"

"Bishop North, you're going to have to cut me some slack here. I told you that her name sounds familiar and that I know the parish, but I simply can't place that woman. Give me something else to help me jog my memory."

"She sings in the choir. She says she met you at a choir party to welcome their new rector."

Suddenly the woman came into view. Sean sat forward in his chair. He almost couldn't contain his excitement. "Now I remember her. Bishop North, that woman is crazy."

The bishop didn't share Sean's enthusiasm. "If that's your defense it won't work. Discrediting your accuser…well, that just won't do."

"But John, you don't understand. She's absolutely certifiable. She's nuts."

"So you do know her?"

"Yes, I remember everything. They invited me to a choir party in that parish after they called the new rector. The woman was so obnoxious. She attached herself to me as soon as I walked in the door. I couldn't shake her all evening. She talked my leg off. Every time I tried to talk to someone else she kept interrupting."

"Did you say anything inappropriate to her?"

"John, listen to me. You've been in this business long enough to have encountered one of these women. She kept trying to hold on to me. She even took my arm a couple of times. It was as though she wanted everyone to think I was her date. When I sat down on the couch she squeezed in between me and another person. The seating was so tight the other person got up and left. She kept touching me on my knee."

"Let me repeat. Did you say anything inappropriate to her? Did you touch her physically?"

"Yes, one time she put her hand on my thigh just a bit too close to the garage so I removed her hand from my leg."

"Did you suggest anything sexual to her?"

"No. No. No. A thousand times no. I never touched her except to remove her hand. I was even a bit rude to her at one point, but nothing worked. I couldn't shake her. I guess the only thing I said to her that could be misconstrued was when she introduced herself to me. I told her she had a beautiful smile."

"So why would she make this accusation that you did?"

Sean threw his hands up in the air and flung himself back into his chair. "Because she's nuts! This is total bullshit. I simply can't believe this crazy woman has put my entire election in jeopardy."

John North began thumbing through the papers in the file again. Then he looked back at Sean. "Okay, let's say that she is unstable. That still doesn't explain why she would go to these lengths to try to destroy your election. Something else happened. I need to know the rest of the story."

Sean buried his face in his hands. "I really can't remember anything else."

"You simply haven't given me enough to negate her accusation. When these accusations are false, spurned lovers or jealous peers have usually made them. Otherwise, I have no choice but to believe they are true."

"What if the person is just plain nuts? Have you considered that as a possibility? Every priest in the Church knows that there are a few looney tunes in every congregation."

"We have to take all accusations seriously."

"Let me see if I understand this. A priest can faithfully serve the church for years. Keep themselves above reproach. Live a life of service that could earn them a seat in heaven next to Francis of Assisi and some obscure person who's not playing with a full deck of cards can destroy it all."

"We have to take every accusation seriously."

"And that's your defense?"

"Sean, we're not getting anywhere. Unless you can remember something else about your encounter with your accuser, my hands are tied."

Sean shook his head. "This is incredible. I simply don't believe this is happening." Sean sat back in his chair and closed his eyes. His heart was sinking with disappointment. Then suddenly he remembered. He jumped to his feet. "Now I remember. That crazy woman followed me to my car after the party. She invited me to follow her to her apartment for a cup of coffee."

"Go on."

"Well, I told her *no*. Then I got in my car and left."

"Did anyone else see you?"

Sean smiled. "Yes, the choirmaster. He called me the next day."

"And?"

"He apologized for the entire choir. He said that woman was a real problem for all the men in the choir. He told me she was a sad soul in so many ways. He described her as needy. She had an inexhaustible need for attention and compliments. He said that he saw her follow me to my car and that she was fit to be tied after I left." Sean smacked himself on his forehead with his hand. "Damn, it's true. No good deed goes unpunished. That was my mistake. I paid her a compliment."

"Okay. Now you've given me something I can work with."

"Didn't you even investigate this woman before you started all this crap?"

"We made some calls."

"And?"

"The rector of the parish described her pretty much as you have."

Now Sean was furious. "And that wasn't enough for you! I just can't believe this. That should have been enough to satisfy you. There was no need to put me through all this."

"As I've told you repeatedly, we have to investigate every accusation."

"Oh, give me a break."

"That's exactly what I am going to do. I am choosing to believe you, but I need you to do one more thing."

"What?"

"I am going to send you to our psychiatrist for another psychological evaluation."

"You've got to be kidding."

"Sean, it's part of the process. It's standard procedure in these situations. I fear that if you want your election process to move forward, you have to do this."

"Fine. I'll do it. But I'm not happy about it."

"It has to be done."

"John, can I ask a favor of you?"

"If I can do it."

"When I am consecrated as the Bishop of Savannah I'd prefer that you not be present."

"Sean, I understand how you feel. Please know I'm just doing my job. After your psychological evaluation I feel confident that I am going to recommend your election stand, but you're forgetting one thing."

"Oh?"

"This woman is still threatening to come to your ordination and vocally object by making her accusation public."

Nausea swept over Sean. He broke out in a cold sweat. He felt like he was going to faint. He put his head between his knees.

chapter 20

WOMEN ARE NOT permitted in the grand ballroom of The Magnolia Club at lunchtime on weekdays. That particular dining room is reserved for gentlemen diners only. Wives of members and their guests are permitted in the front parlor of the club. Unlike the grand ballroom, which can seat several hundred people at one time, the front parlor has a maximum seating of seventy-five. Two large crystal chandeliers accent the room. The wall is lined with windows. The opposing wall has four very large brass mirrors hanging on it. The combined effect gives the room an appearance of being much larger. Still, it is an intimate room and ideal for small wedding receptions, rehearsal dinners and as a luncheon venue for ladies of social position.

"I would like that table at the far end of the room next to the window." Mrs. Gordon Smythe instructed Clarence, the maître d'.

"Yes'm, Mrs. Smythe. I'd sure like to do that fer ya, but the club manager, he told me to start seat'n folks from the front of the room to the back. Unless we get a big crowd today we won't even be sit'n people at those tables down there."

"Clarence, I am not the least bit interested in what the club manager has told you to do. Mrs. Alexander-Drummond and I want the table at the far end next to the window. We have some important matters to discuss of a confidential manner that we simply don't want prying ears to hear."

"Yes'm. I do it fer ya but I 'm a gonna get in trouble."

"If the club manager gives you any grief whatsoever, you send him to me."

"Yes'm."

"My goodness, Mary Alice, what is all the secrecy? I just thought you invited me to lunch for a little girl talk."

"I only wish that were the case. I really need to talk to you about a matter of some urgency, but let's order first."

After each of the ladies had ordered the shrimp salad and sweet tea, Almeda scanned the room. "Just take a look around, Mary Alice. Look at how beautifully everyone is dressed."

Mary Alice turned in her chair so that she could observe the other diners. "Yes, everyone is dressed immaculately."

"Look at the number of ladies wearing gloves. Don't you miss wearing your gloves?"

"Oh, I still wear my dress gloves on occasion. It just depends on the event and my attire."

Almeda smiled as her mind flashed to the distant past. "Do you remember when no lady would think of going to church without wearing her gloves? The Sunday bulletin always carried a reminder for us to remove one glove before receiving the blessed bread in our hand."

"Of course I remember, but those days are long gone."

"Do they have to be forgotten? We're making progress on getting women to wear head coverings at worship. Don't you think we could do the same with gloves?"

"Almeda, I hate to disturb your hopes, but frankly, I don't think very many of the young women today even own a pair of gloves."

"You're probably right. I guess I should just be happy with small victories. By the way, where is your sidekick? I thought for sure that Martha would be joining us."

"No, I didn't invite her. When I tell you what I have to report, then you'll understand why I couldn't ask her to dine with us."

"Oh?"

After their shrimp salads had been served, Mary Alice lowered her voice. "You've become quite fond of the rector, haven't you?"

Almeda smiled. "I love him like he were one of my sons. I love his beautiful wife and those precious children. I think it's safe to say my affections go far beyond fondness, but I think you already knew that."

"I did. I need to tell you a couple of things. First, I've really been feeling bad about the way our church has treated Misturh Austin and his family. I particularly feel bad about the way I treated him when he first arrived."

"Have you told him that?"

"In my own way."

"No, have you told him in the words you just used with me?"

Mary Alice put her fork down and gestured for the waiter to clear her plate. "I fear not, but I plan on doing so as soon as he returns...if he returns. Do you think he will return to First Church from his sabbatical?"

"Horace and I believe that he will, but I guess there's always the chance that he won't, and who could blame him?"

"I guess that's the other thing I need to tell you, but before I do I want you to know that I am just heartsick about my behavior. I'm even more embarrassed about the behavior of some of the folks in our church."

"I know you are, Mary Alice. Now what is it that you need to tell me?"

Mary Alice waited for the waiter to clear Almeda's plate. "Would you ladies like some dessert? I needs to tell you that the pastry chef has whipped up some red velvet cake. I saw it in the kitchen and it shore do look mighty tasty."

"That sounds wonderful." Almeda nodded. "I haven't baked a red velvet cake since Christmas. Yes, bring me a piece with a cup of coffee."

"None for me, but do bring me a cup of coffee." When the waiter walked away, Mary Alice continued. "You know the Confederate Honor Society held their annual ball a couple of weeks ago."

"Yes. When Chadsworth was alive I used to attend with him. Since his death my invitations were withdrawn. I was unable to demonstrate that any of my ancestors fought for the Confederacy. Now mind you they did. I'm told that my great grandfather fought side by side with General Stonewall Jackson himself. I just haven't been able to get the necessary documents."

Mary Alice's eyes grew large. "Almeda, you still wouldn't want to go to that event, would you?"

"Of course not." Almeda chuckled. "The only way that they would let us in is if my Horace agreed to be one of the waiters."

"Almeda, you're just awful." Mary Alice had to cover her mouth, she was giggling so hard.

"Why did you bring up the Confederate Honor Society?"

"Martha Dexter told me about a conversation her husband had with Colonel Mitchell, Gary Hendrix and Tom Barnhardt."

"I can't stand those two men."

"Which two?"

"Hendrix and that Barnhardt. They think that they are the smartest people in Falls City. The two of them are a couple of real skunks if you ask me. What are they up to now?"

"Howard told Martha that they've all agreed to separate the school from the parish."

"Personally, I've never been a fan of the school. My boys went there and they were treated something awful by some of those teachers. They did nothing to help them, so we pulled our boys out of that so-called school and sent them to Woodberry Forest."

"I remember all that. So it wouldn't bother you if they pulled the school away."

"Not in the least, but there are some pretty powerful people at First Church that are invested in the parish continuing to own it."

"I agree. I think there's going to have to be some well placed funerals before that can happen."

"I can name those folks for you right now."

"No need. Howard told Martha that they all think that Misturh Austin will oppose them if they try to do it."

"I agree. Some of those folks are counting on him to do that very thing. If he lets them down, he'll have even more trouble than he could possibly survive. You just don't want to cross some of those men. No, I'm sure they're counting on him to maintain parish ownership. After they're all dead it will be another matter, but if any rector betrays them while they're alive he'll have more grief than he can ever survive."

"Well, it may be that Misturh Austin will not have a choice in the matter. Howard and the other three have all agreed to oppose him. If he doesn't go along, they're going to renew their efforts to get rid of him once and for all."

Almeda felt her anger stir. "Martha reported all this to you?"

"She did, but please don't tell her I told you."

"I see. Well, if those four so-called gentlemen renew attacks on Steele and his family, they will have stirred up a hornet's nest. I will personally oppose them. I will join with the forces that want to keep the school under the parish. I know those men and they will not have it any other way. I see no reason why Barnhardt and that entire crew can't go the way of Ned Boone and the Idles."

"You think the new bishop will go along with that?"

"Mary Alice, I promise you that he will." Just then the waiter brought Almeda her red velvet cake. "Now, let's talk about something more pleasant. I want to enjoy this cake. You sure you don't want a bite?"

chapter 21

EVERYTHING HAD BEEN going so well at First Church. Horace Drummond couldn't have been happier. Other than a confrontation with Gary Hendricks over the school at last month's vestry meeting, everything had been smooth. Horace even surmised that the confrontation with Gary had been a good thing. The vestry amended the by-laws to allow the rector to name the senior warden and the vestry to elect from their own number the junior warden. This was a good thing. Attendance at worship had not declined in Steele's absence. It was holding steady. People were still paying their pledges. There were the usual number of weddings and funerals, but he was able to share those with Mother Graystone and the parish deacon. They were more than willing to assist him. The deacon was carrying the lion's share of the pastoral calling on the long-term shut-ins. She didn't complain one bit and kept Horace informed of any members he needed to visit. He counted himself fortunate to have these two wonderful clergy to assist him.

The Sunday worship services had run just as smoothly. The vergers did an excellent job of covering the details for each service. The acolytes were well trained and managed efficiently by the vergers. Perfection didn't even come close to describing the work of the altar guild each Sunday. And the ushers, under Colonel Mitchell, exercised their duties with military precision. The organist had attempted to run some hymns in on Horace that the National Cathedral Choir would have struggled to sing. He had to confront him on those and veto what Horace considered to be hymns totally unsuited for congregational singing. Otherwise the choir had continued to inspire the congregation's worship.

This Sunday, however, left a lot to be desired. It began before he even made it to the sacristy. A tearful Barbara Duncan confronted him. He couldn't tell if she was upset, angry, or both. She met him in the parking lot as he was getting out of his car. She was waving the Sunday worship leaflet at him. "I can't believe this. This is terrible. What's wrong with you people?"

Horace attempted to calm her. "I don't understand. I don't know why you're upset. You've got to help me understand."

Tears streamed down her face as she yelled at Horace. She was pounding her pointed finger on the Sunday worship leaflet. "Here... right here! Look at this! Read this!" She was now screaming at Horace.

Horace took the bulletin from her. She continued to point at the line she wanted him to read. *The flowers on the altar today are given to the glory of God in thanksgiving for Mister Albert Duncan's corporate promotion.*

Horace still didn't understand. "Albert Duncan is your grandfather. Correct?"

She wiped the tears from her face and nodded. Horace checked the spelling. Everything appeared to be spelled correctly. "Are the flowers on the altar not the ones that you requested? Do they not suit you?"

"No, it's not the flowers. The flowers are perfectly lovely."

Horace looked at the bulletin again. He was still confused as to why the woman was upset. "Aren't you happy about your grandfather's promotion? Does it require him to move?"

The woman's face changed from anger to disbelief. "Doctor Drummond, my grandfather didn't get a promotion. He died!"

"Oh my gosh, how could this have happened?"

"I called the office and told the secretary how I wanted the bulletin to read...she reached in her pocket and brought out a sheet of paper. Here. This is what I told her to write in the bulletin. *The flowers are given to the glory of God in thanksgiving for Mister Albert Duncan's promotion to the communion of saints.*

"Wow. I am so sorry. Would it help if I correct the bulletin when I do the announcements? And then next week I'll make sure that we print the correction. Would that be acceptable?"

The woman nodded and then she began to laugh. Horace was at a loss as to what to do. "Are you okay?"

The woman composed herself. "If I didn't know better I would think that my grandfather manipulated this entire thing. It would be just like him. He was always pulling practical jokes on us."

"I'm sorry that I never knew him."

Oh, you would have liked him. He was quite the character. When he was dying my mother asked him where he wanted to be buried. He'd never bought cemetery property. My grandma's ashes had been distributed in the ocean. She so loved the seaside. Do you know what he said when my mother asked him where he wanted to be buried?"

Horace shook his head.

"He looked up at my mother from his death bed and said, 'Surprise me!'"

"He sounds just like the kind of guy I would have enjoyed. Are we all right?"

The woman nodded. "Thanks. Thanks for taking care of this."

Things didn't get any better once the service had started. The thurifer decided he wanted to try some figure eights with the incense pot during the processional. On his first attempt the thurible opened, dropping hot coals on the carpet. The procession had to be stopped so the ushers could spray the carpet with fire extinguishers. Horace knew for sure that he'd be hearing from the anti-incense crowd on that one.

The hymn before the morning Gospel was an all-time favorite of the congregation. The organist had offered an alternative. Horace had overruled him and insisted that the familiar hymn be sung. The organist started the hymn and then went off-key for a couple of bars before regaining the hymn as written. Horace was certain the organist had done it on purpose. The interesting thing was that the congregation and choir had followed the organist off-key and then regained the melody when he returned. The entire place roared with laughter and continued to sing.

Mother Graystone was the preacher of the day and delivered a wonderful sermon that seemed to have everyone's approval. The creed, prayers of the people and the confession all went without a hitch. Horace made his announcements. The offering was received and presented at the altar. Horace began the Sursum Corda.

"The Lord be with you."

The people responded, "And with your spirit."

"Lift up your hearts." Horace proclaimed.

"We lift them up to the Lord." The people responded with enthusiasm.

Just then one of the acolytes passed out and fell face down on the sanctuary floor. Horace looked at the verger and nodded for him to remove the acolyte. The verger stood frozen. Horace was exasperated. He shouted at the verger. "Get that acolyte out of here."

And then right on cue, the congregation shouted. "It's meet and right so to do!".

⚜

chapter 22

VIRGINIA MUDD STARED at her checkbook. Her rent was due and she simply didn't have enough money to make the payment. She had gone through all the money that Henry had given her in the divorce. Virginia walked into her bedroom and looked through her closet. She had no formal dresses left. She used to have one entire closet set aside in the house on River Street for formal wear. Those were the dresses she'd wear to the cotillion, debutante ball and the many black tie events. She'd placed them all in the consignment shop. She had none left. Virginia sorted through the remaining clothes. She needed to find a few more items she could sell, but there just was nothing.

Desperate for money, she opened the jewelry box she'd hidden underneath her bed. She'd already pawned the pieces she felt she could part with. She shook her head. She only had a few pieces left and she didn't want to take them to the pawn dealer. Virginia returned to her little breakfast table and compared the numbers on her bank statement with those on her checkbook. They reconciled. She had to get the money for the rent.

Virginia picked up the telephone. She started to call Alicia but replaced the phone in its cradle. She hadn't talked to Alicia in months. Her sponsor and both of her support groups had convinced her to cut off all communications with Alicia. Virginia knew they were right. Not only had Alicia virtually blessed her adultery with Jacque by providing them with her lake house, but she also helped her manufacture cover stories to tell Henry. Her group told her that Alicia was not a nice person. Others used even stronger words to describe Alicia's behavior. Alicia was also her source for pot and other drugs.

Since the traumatic event she'd had with Craig, she had resolved to take her sobriety seriously. She knew that she got off easy with that mad man. He could have really hurt her, raped her, and worse. She was working her twelve steps with an even stronger resolution than ever before. She did ask for a new sponsor. She'd had to confess to her group that she was sexually attracted to her sponsor. She was given a new sponsor. Barbara was a lot harder on her than her previous sponsor, but she was always there when Virginia needed her.

Her glass was empty so she poured herself more sweet tea. Virginia stared out her little kitchen window that was above her sink. She felt the tears streaming down her cheeks. She just couldn't believe that her life had turned out like this. If only Henry had been more forgiving. After all, they'd taken marriage vows for better or worse. He'd promised to love her until death. Every Sunday at First Church they were reminded that God loves us and forgives us. We're supposed to do the same. Why couldn't Henry forgive her?

Virginia shook herself back to reality. She wiped her face with a dishcloth. "That's drunk thinking," she muttered. She knew if she was going to find serenity she had to accept responsibility for what she'd done. She'd messed up her life. It wasn't Henry's fault. She had no one to blame but herself.

Back at the table she still had to figure out a way to pay her rent. She thought about calling the pastor of her new church to see if he would help her. He'd done so once before. She didn't have enough money to buy her daughters the presents she wanted them to have last Christmas. The pastor gave her some money out of the emergency fund to allow her to buy the gifts. Maybe he would help her pay her rent. But then there would be next month's rent and the month after. "Oh my God, I am going to be homeless." Virginia's body shook as she dropped her head onto the table and allowed the panic to pour out of her.

When Virginia was finally able to compose herself she knew what she had to do. She picked up the telephone and punched in the number. She had dialed it so many times before.

"Mister Mudd."

Henry looked up from the case file that was spread across his desk.

"Mister Mudd, your ex-wife is on the telephone."

"Tell her I am in a meeting."

"She says it's an emergency. She has to talk with you right now. She said to tell you that it's a matter of life and death."

Henry nodded. "Which line is she on?"

"Three."

"Virginia, what's the emergency?"

"Henry, I have to see you. I need to see you as quickly as possible."

"What's this about? You said it's a matter of life and death."

"It is, Henry, but I need to tell you in person. I don't want to discuss it over the telephone."

Henry sat silent for a few minutes. One of the last people in this world he wanted to look at was Virginia. He certainly didn't want to discuss anything with her. "Okay, Virginia. I suppose I have something I need to tell you. I owe you that much. I've got to be in court in one hour and I'll be there the rest of the day. I have an obligation tonight so my day is pretty well booked. Tell you what, I'll meet you for breakfast in the morning."

"Where? Can we go someplace we won't be seen?"

Henry thought for a minute. "You know the truck stop out on the freeway?"

"Yes."

"Of course you do." Henry smirked. "You're probably quite familiar with it."

Henry's words pierced Virginia. She felt herself flinch. "Henry, please."

"I'll meet you there at eight o'clock."

"Thank you, Henry. I'll see you then."

"There's no reason to thank me, Virginia. You may not want to hear what I have to tell you." Then Henry abruptly placed his telephone back on the cradle.

chapter 23

SEAN HAD SPENT the night in a hotel just a few blocks from the Church Center in New York City. He'd thought about going to a gay bar to pass away the evening but decided that wasn't wise. The last thing he needed was for some babbling queen to see him. He decided in favor of just having dinner in his room and watching a movie on television. His anger still raged inside him. He was angry at the crazy nut that had started all this. He was angry with Bishop North that he hadn't just dismissed the entire issue after he'd talked to the rector of Holy Cross. The fact that the rector thought the woman was crazy should have been more than enough. One unstable woman had put his election on hold and cost the Church unnecessary expense.

The offices of Doctor David Stein were within walking distance of the hotel and were literally in the shadow of the Church Center. Doctor Stein could not have been more textbook. He was wearing a dark suit with a vest. His face was framed with dark rimmed glasses. He was sporting a dark goatee and mustache.

"Please sit down, Canon Evans. I've gone through your file. The pastoral care office has basically asked me to do a follow up interview."

"Okay. What do you need to know?"

"Well, it's not quite that simple. I'd like for you to tell me how you are feeling right now."

"Quite frankly, I'm pissed."

"Go on."

"Doctor Stein, you've read the file. A woman that most likely could keep a psychiatrist in a new Mercedes every year is responsible for all of this."

"And that makes you angry?"

Sean gently shook his head in disbelief. *And now I get to play echo with a shrink.* "Wouldn't it make you angry?"

"Let me ask you. Is there anything you could have done to have prevented all this?"

"What?"

"Could you have behaved in a manner that would have kept the woman from accusing you?"

"You've got to be kidding. This is all bullshit. The woman is nuts. She attached herself to me at that party and in spite of my best efforts I couldn't shake her. When she asked me to go to her apartment I gave her a firm *no*. Now tell me, in the same circumstance, what would you have done? Please…I'm open to suggestions."

The psychiatrist scribbled some notes on his pad. "Do you think this experience has been sufficiently traumatic so as to impair your ability to function as the Bishop of Savannah?"

"Doctor Stein, I'm not traumatized. I'm angry. I want to get all of this over with so that I can go to Savannah and do the job I was elected to do."

"Okay. Tell me. Why do you think you should be a bishop?"

"First, I believe God has called me to that ministry. My election has confirmed that feeling for me. Second, I have a ministry vision for the diocese and I am anxious to implement it."

The psychiatrist made more notes. "Let's go back to the accusation. Is this the first time anyone has accused you of sexual misconduct?"

"What? I don't believe this. Of course it is and I don't consider it to even be a credible accusation. I did nothing. You're a psychiatrist; surely you can spot a nut when you see one."

Doctor Stein chuckled. "Oh, Canon Evans, if only it were that easy. I fear that if we were to let all the current patients in the mental hospitals out to roam the streets, we'd never be able to get the right ones back in."

Sean relaxed in his chair and nodded his agreement with a couple of chuckles of his own. "I think you've got that one right."

"I would like for you to be a little more specific about your encounter with your accuser."

"Gosh, I don't know what else I can tell you. I think I've already told Bishop North everything I could remember. Didn't he send you a copy of his report?"

"Yes, I've read his report, but I'd like to follow up on a hunch. I am going to ask you some specific questions. You tell me if any of these apply to this woman."

"Okay. I'll do my best, but remember I was only around her one evening."

"Did you feel she exhibited a seductive or flirtatious behavior?"

"Absolutely. She started coming on to me soon after I met her. She immediately started looking deep in my eyes."

Doctor Stein wrote his response on a legal pad. "Did you think she was sincere?"

"No. I thought she was acting. I felt like she was trying to say things to me she thought I wanted to hear. She kept exaggerating her compliments to me. They were so overdone that I knew they weren't sincere. She was definitely testing me to see if I was a player."

"What about her appearance? Would you describe her as overly concerned with it?"

Sean reflected back to the woman. "She was dressed to the nines. She did ask me a couple of times if her lipstick was smeared."

"Did she show concern for others at the party?"

"Hell, no. She locked onto me. It was as though she thought we were the only ones there. When another person came up to talk to me you could tell she resented it. If the other person was a woman she immediately froze them out in an effort to get rid of them. It's all coming back to me. I simply couldn't shake the woman."

Doctor Stein was studying the notes he had written on the legal pad. "I know this will require you to do some speculation, but how do you think she would handle rejection or criticism?"

"Doctor Stein, have you not been listening? That's what brought all this on. I rejected her flirtations. Where are you going with this?"

"Sean, you've described a woman with a distorted self-image. Her self-esteem is totally dependent on the approval of others. Such women often behave inappropriately. They have boundary issues. By that, I mean they don't have any boundaries. If they see something or someone they want, they take it. They have little regard for how their behavior will impact another. They often act out sexually in an effort to seek approval from men. Men can also behave in that manner but the particular diagnosis I am considering is more common in women."

"What diagnosis are you considering?"

Doctor Stein reviewed his notes once again. "Canon Evans, have you ever heard of Histrionic Personality Disorder?"

"I've heard of it."

"Your answers, along with the descriptions of this woman's behavior supplied by her rector and choir director, have pretty much confirmed my suspicion. Of course, I'd need to meet the woman and spend some time with her before making a conclusive diagnosis."

"So you think she's histrionic?"

"At the very least she has Borderline Personality Disorder. I really think that after reviewing all the information I have received I'm leaning toward histrionic."

"Wow. What causes it?"

"Oh, we really don't know for certain. The prevailing opinion is that they're simply one of the losers in the genetic lottery. Other professionals lean more toward environment. Studies indicate that a common thread is that they've grown up in a family where they did not receive a lot of positive reinforcement. They grew up craving compliments and reassurance. I fear unaffectionate mothers get the major blame. It leaves them with a bottomless pit that simply can't be filled. That can also lead to addictive behaviors. I tend to think that it's a combination of both heredity and environment."

"And you think that's what I'm dealing with in this woman? Are you going to put that in your report?"

"I am."

"Before we bring this interview to a close I need to ask you a question you've already been asked in this process several times."

"Okay."

"Have you ever done anything that if made public would be an embarrassment to you and the Church?"

"No."

"You're sure about that?"

"Look, I am a normal healthy male. Sure, I did some stupid things as a teenager and in college, but since entering the seminary I've tried to keep my skirts clean."

"About being a normal healthy male. You're single. Do you date?"

"No."

"You're going to have to say more."

"No. I'm not interested. I am a member of a religious order and I've taken a vow of celibacy."

"Did you ever date?"

"I had a few dates in high school and college."

"With women?"

"Of course with women. What are you suggesting?"

"In a minute. Did you have sex with any of those women?"

"One."

"And?"

"That's all. I did it and I decided it's something I can live without."

"Are you gay?"

"I told you I've taken vows of celibacy for religious reasons. I think that I can serve God and the Church better if I'm not responsible for a wife and children. You did see that I grew up Roman Catholic. Every priest I knew when I was younger was celibate. I admired them for their ministries and the sacrifices they made for them."

Doctor Stein had been writing on his pad the entire time Sean was speaking. It was as though he was trying to record every word. "Canon Evans, have you ever had sex with a man?"

"That again. I thought I told you that I'm celibate."

"You did."

"I'm just curious. What would happen if I had told you that I have had sex with a man? Remember I told you that I am celibate. What happens to the men that tell you they have done that? Do you void their elections?"

The psychiatrist stared a Sean for a long time in silence. "Well, that's not my call. I only do evaluations and report my findings to the Office of Pastoral Care down the street. I can tell you that I have had men in here that confessed to being gay and I had to report it. I think your church requires them to be celibate before their elections are approved."

"You said your church. Aren't you an Episcopalian?"

"Sean, I'm a Jew."

"Well, I didn't see that one coming."

"My name didn't give it away?"

"I'm sorry. I guess I was just focusing on myself."

"Now that you understand my role in all of this. I'm going to ask you again. Are you gay?"

chapter 24

STEELE AND TRAVIS were sitting on the floor in the living room of the beach house. They were playing Candyland. Amanda was lying in her baby bouncer on the floor next to Steele. She was watching the two of them as though she completely understood the game. Randi put her book down so that she could watch them. "You realize you have a couple of appendages."

Steele looked at her and smiled. "One of them follows me everywhere I go. I've almost had to start showering with him."

"Even Amanda follows you with her eyes when you come into a room. She starts waving her arms and legs wanting you to pick her up."

"I know."

"They like having you around. Steele, I like having you around. This is really nice."

"I have to admit I could get used to it. I am finally feeling like I'm beginning to relax."

"I can tell. Just look at you. In just a few days you've started putting on some weight. Your skin even looks healthier. I think we'd better really give all this some serious thought."

"Daddy, it's your turn." Travis was pulling on his daddy's shirt.

"Okay. Sorry, I was talking to mommy." After Steele had taken his turn he looked back at Randi. "What did you have in mind?"

"Just think about what you will be going back to if you decide to return to First Church."

"Go on."

"Steele, you know as well as I do that you were exhausted practically all the time. You worked at the church all day and then when you came home at night we often had to leave the kids with a sitter to go to a dinner party or you were out at a night meeting."

"I know."

"Even if you were at home at night it seemed like you were on the telephone or had your face buried in books doing research for your next sermon."

"It's all a part of the job."

"I know that, honey, but do you feel like it's worth it? I mean, just look what the past few years at First Church have done to you. Look at what it almost did to us."

"We knew that we'd have to make sacrifices. I didn't try to hide that from you before I asked you to marry me. Remember, we talked about it."

"I'm not blaming you. I just didn't think it would be like this. I've heard of the glass house my entire life. I've heard other clergy spouses talk about the challenge of the glass house. I guess I just never really understood. I don't suppose anyone can until they've actually lived in one."

"Are you saying you don't want me to go back to First Church? Randi, if that's what you really want, I won't do it."

"I don't think we have to make a decision just yet, but I want us to really think this through."

"We're going to. I promise."

"Have you thought about what it's going to be like when Travis and Amanda start school? Or how about when they become teenagers? Steele, you won't be able to do Indian Guides with either one of them. Most all those activities are over the weekends. Or let's say Travis wants to play a sport, you'll miss most all his games. You have retreats and weddings on weekends. And what about Christmas? You'll be working. It just seems to me you're always exhausted."

"Randi, I have thought about all that. I know that I'm going to miss a lot of things with them but I'm determined to make it up to them in other ways. I will make time for my children."

"Well then, what about us? Steele, your mind is always working. You get these distant looks on your face. Your body is with me but your mind is someplace else. I was married to you for three years before I realized I hadn't done something wrong. I thought you were mad at me. Now I know you're just working on your sermon or some church project in your head. But I feel neglected. I feel lonely when you're home but you're not home."

"I'm sorry. I never wanted you to feel that way. I wish you'd told me about this before now. I'll try to do better."

"I know you will, but I guess I'm afraid you won't be able to. I think if we go back it's just a matter of time until it starts all over again. I know it sounds like I'm whining. There are plenty of people that have it worse off than we do. But Steele, this is our life. We've got to ask ourselves if the sacrifices are worth it."

Travis had lost interest in Candyland and ran into his bedroom in search of something else to play. Amanda had drifted off to sleep.

"Let's talk about money. We're using some of my trust fund just to meet our everyday expenses. We've already gone through everything you were able to accumulate before we got married. I know that we're among the fortunate clergy that actually have something to fall back on. But Steele, we should be saving and investing, but we can't."

"I know you're right. And it doesn't seem fair."

"No it doesn't. You work hard. You work long hours and you've done a great job, but they seem to resent every penny they pay you."

"It probably won't get much better, but I have been given some raises."

"Cost of living raises, Steele. What about merit increases? You've quadrupled their ministry budget. Your salary is not much more than it was when we arrived."

"We did get a good housing allowance so we could buy our own home."

"Steele, you almost had to get a lawyer to get them to honor the terms of their own written contract. They didn't do one cent more than they had agreed to do when they called you here."

"Randi, I didn't go into the ministry to make a lot of money. That was a conscious decision on my part. We talked about that before we got married. Remember?"

"I remember. I guess I just didn't realize how hard it was going to be."

Steele stood and walked over to the couch. He sat down next to Randi and put both of his arms around her. "We don't have to go back to First Church. I don't have to be a parish priest. We can sell the house in Falls City and move any place we want. I can find another job that won't require me to work all the time. I'm positive I can find one that will pay me better. Is that what you really want?"

"Could we move back to Oklahoma? Our parents live there. Wouldn't it be nice to live close to our families again? We could go home."

Steele kissed her on the forehead. "Yes, it would be nice. Tell me truthfully. Is that what you want to do?"

A tear streamed down Randi's cheek. She nodded.

⚜

chapter 25

HARLAN MCMURRAY WAS meeting with Ned Boone, Judith and Elmer Idle in his office. "We've been following the plan you outlined for us, Ned, but I fear that it might not be working."

"Oh?" Ned looked surprised.

"Well, a couple of us have been going to the session meetings, but the pastor complimented us for coming. He said that he was so pleased to see us take such an interest in the work of the church. All the session members thanked us for coming."

"They didn't ask why you were there?"

"No, they just kept thanking us for coming."

Elmer scratched his head. "What about the cottage meetings?"

'We've only been able to put together one meeting. I held it at my house. I had about a dozen people show up."

Elmer and Ned gently shook their heads. "Was everyone on board with getting rid of your preacher?"

"For certain. There was not a dissenting voice present. We are all of one mind. The man needs to go. Everyone agreed to write letters to the presbytery up in Savannah saying as much."

"Well, that's a good start. Did you ask each of them to host a cottage meeting and invite like-minded people to attend?"

Harlan wrinkled his forehead. "That's the hitch. None of those present knew anyone else that they could invite."

"I thought you told us that there were quite a number of people that wanted him to leave."

"That was certainly my impression but I could have been wrong."

Judith's eyes brightened. "I've been going to the Wednesday morning ladies Bible study. There are over a hundred women that attend that study. I have to tell you that it appears to me that every one of them is just crazy about the pastor. Some of his teachings come up in practically every lesson. I haven't heard any unhappiness with him."

"That's sure a different report than I've been getting. " Harlan rebutted. "My wife and her friends can't stand the man. They won't even go to that Bible study. My wife says that he has all those women fooled."

Judith murmured. "Well, I have to tell you I kind of like his sermons. He preaches the Bible. We didn't get that at First Church. Your preacher takes the scriptures and makes them come to life. I like that. I think that's what the women in the Bible study like as well."

"Pablum. Sentimental dribble. That's all I hear coming out of the man's mouth." Harlan couldn't hide his irritation.

Elmer put his arm around Judith. "Gentlemen, you're going to have to excuse my wife. She's such a good-hearted person she always tries to find the best in everyone she knows. I love that about her but that's also the reason she often ends up disappointed and hurt. She always wants to give the preacher the benefit of the doubt. "

Judith shut her eyes and began moving her mouth in prayer. The three men watched her for a minute. Harlan interrupted the silence. "Ned, did your detective discover anything?"

Ned nodded. "I fear he did. It's pretty nasty. Your preacher may have the majority of the congregation fooled, but he's living with an ugly secret."

Judith's opened her eyes. "You don't mean it, Ned?"

"I regret that I do. In fact, it's so disgusting that I don't even want to tell you about it."

"Will it make him resign?" Harlan asked eagerly.

"Oh, if what my detectives discovered ever becomes public, a resignation will just be the beginning."

"It's that bad, Ned?" Elmer asked.

"It's just about the worst thing that a preacher; no, it's the worse thing that any man could do."

"Wow." Harlan let out a low whistle. "This sounds serious."

Ned nodded. "It is."

Harlan snapped his fingers. "I knew it. You know the first time I met that man I didn't like him. I just knew that there was something amiss. He may have this congregation fooled but he never fooled me. Are you going to tell us what your detective found?"

"No, I'm not. I think it would be best if an independent source discovered it. The best thing we can do is let them know where to look."

"Oh." Harlan leaned toward Ned. "Where should I look?"

"I don't want you to discover this information. If I read the congregation correctly, they already know that you're opposed to the preacher. The fact that you've held the only cottage meeting to plot his demise won't go unnoticed by his supporters. No, we've got to figure another way."

"Tell me what you're thinking." Harlan encouraged Ned.

"I read in the worship leaflet last Sunday that the auditors are coming in next week to do the annual audit of your books."

"That's correct. My brother-in-law is the chair of the audit committee."

Ned smiled. "Do you think you could get him to expand the audit?"

"To include what? Do you suspect the preacher is stealing money?"

Ned shook his head. "No, his transgressions are not financial. We just need your auditors to audit his computer."

"His computer?"

"Not just his. We need them to audit all the computers. It's standard operating procedure for most audits. We just need to make sure that they do an audit of his as well."

"What are they looking for?"

"Harlan, they just need to have a look at the websites he's been visiting. Make sure they have a look at any documents he might have hidden inside an innocent looking file."

"It shouldn't be a problem. I think that I can get my brother-in-law to authorize it."

Ned smiled. "Just assure him that if he's worried about any additional expense, you have a donor willing to pay for it. Just tell him it's a member that wants to make sure that the church gets a thorough audit."

When Ned got back to his home office, he picked up the telephone and punched in a number. When he heard the man answer he had just one question. "Is it done?'

"I've personally taken care of it."

A very satisfied Ned Boone hung up the telephone and poured himself a celebratory drink.

chapter 26

HENRY AND DELILAH had just finished a romantic dinner at The Spanish Moss Inn. The old antebellum house had at one time been the residence of one of the most prestigious families in Falls City. The last person to live there was a bachelor great-great grandson of the original owners. Since there were no more survivors, the house was sold and the proceeds given to the various charities specified in his final will and testament. The house was converted to a bed and breakfast by a young couple from Augusta. They converted the large living room to a piano bar. Meals were served in the dining room that had been enlarged by removing the wall separating it from the servant's bedroom and laundry room. The screened back porch provided yet another alternative for dining. There were also tables in the gardens surrounding the house for those who preferred to eat outside. Dinner was open to the public with advance reservations.

Following dinner, Henry asked Delilah to take a stroll with him through the gardens behind the Inn. They walked hand in hand, admiring the beautiful flowers and shrubs that were accented by landscape lighting. The camellias were in bloom. Hanging baskets filled to overflowing with brightly colored annuals decorated the lower branches of the trees. Seated on a bench near a large water fountain, Henry put his arm around Delilah and pulled her close to him. "Dee, honey. Do you have any idea just how much I love you?"

Delilah looked up at him and kissed him. "And do you have any idea just how much I love you?" She then nestled her head in his arm. "How do you think it's going with my girls?"

Delilah lifted her head from his arm and positioned herself so that she could look at him. "Henry, I love your girls. We have a wonderful time together. I plan to take each of them out individually and together as often as I can. I think they trust me. They tell me things…well…you don't need to know what they tell me. Let's just say it's girl talk."

Henry squeezed her hand. "I thought as much. They talk about you all the time. It's Delilah this and Delilah that. I think they've become really fond of you."

"I'm a realist, Henry. I know that I can never replace their mother, but I can be nurturing. I can be their friend."

"I think you already are." Henry sat watching the water flow over the fountain in silence. "You mentioned their mother. I need to tell you something."

"Yes."

"Honey, it's absolutely essential that we not have any secrets from one another. Virginia had a life that I knew nothing about. She kept a lot of secrets. I never want that kind of marriage again."

Dee felt her stomach do a flip. "I know. I want that too." Delilah wondered if this would be a good time to tell Henry her secret. She so desperately wanted to tell him. She needed to tell him.

"Dee, I'm having breakfast with Virginia in the morning."

A look of disbelief washed over Delilah's face. "Did you invite her?"

"Of course not. You have nothing to worry about. There's no reason for even a splinter of worry. Frankly, I never want to see the woman's face again as long as I live. She called me."

"What do you think she wants?"

"Knowing Virginia, she's run through all her money and wants me to give her more."

"Do you want to do that?"

"Not one thin dime. If I give her money this time, she'll just blow through it and come back time and time again for more. Believe me, I now know her in a way that I never did when I was married to her."

"Do you have to give her money? I mean…under the terms of your divorce would you have to?"

"No. The divorce settlement is final. She can't reopen it."

"I guess it's none of my business, but Henry, why did you agree to meet her?"

"Two things. First, she is the mother of my daughters. As you know, the girls are pretty angry with her. I really want to do what I can do to mend their relationship. Virginia is going to have to do her part and I'm going to encourage the girls."

"What can you say to them?"

"I'm just gong to keep reminding them that she is their mother. She gave them life. I'm going to tell them that I want them to at least have a cordial if not warm relationship with her. I want them to do it for themselves as much as they do it for Virginia. If they don't, there will come a day after she's dead that they'll really regret it."

"Henry, you're a good man."

"I don't know about all that, but I'm glad you think so."

"You said you had two things you wanted to tell her."

Henry took Delilah's hand again and squeezed it. "I want to tell her about you."

"Are you sure? "

"I'm sure. How would you feel about formally meeting all my friends?"

Delilah patted her hands together. "I'd love to. What did you have in mind?"

"I want to have a cocktail party. I want to invite all my friends."

"I think that would be wonderful."

"Do you think you and the girls could plan it together? I mean, I think it would work best if the three of you were the hostesses."

"I just know we'll have so much fun doing it. Is there anything in particular you want me to wear or do?"

"Dee, I just want you to be yourself. I've never seen you wear anything that didn't make you look absolutely ravishing."

Delilah beamed. "Oh Henry, I'm so excited."

"I am too." Henry looked at his watch. "I still have a little work to do on the case I'm litigating right now. Would you mind if I drove you home early?"

"Not at all." Delilah looked past Henry at the fountain, lost in thought.

"What's on your mind, pretty lady?"

"I know it's none of my business, but would you call me after your breakfast with Virginia in the morning?"

"That's exactly what I'd intended to do. My business is your business. I won't have it any other way. Remember, I don't want there to be any secrets between us."

Delilah nodded. She needed to share her secret with Henry and she wanted to tell him right now.

"I hate to rush you, but I really do have a lot of work to do. I want to get home in time to tuck the girls in." He stood and extended his hand to her.

Delilah nodded.

❧❧

chapter 27

STEELE WAS SITTING on the porch overlooking the beach and ocean. He was enjoying one of the several pleasures that he had rediscovered on his sabbatical. He was leisurely reading the morning paper. He looked up and spotted Bishop Powers on the beach walking towards him. A very tall slender man dressed in a blue and white seersucker suit accompanied him. The man was dressed as though he had just come from church. He had on a starched white shirt, a red bow tie, white buck shoes and he was wearing a plantation owner's hat. Steele had never seen anyone go for a walk on the beach dressed so formally. Bishop Powers was shouting up at Steele and waving for him to come down. "Steele, come down here. I want you to meet this fellow."

Steele opened the screen door and went down the steps. He extended his hand to the bishop and then to the man. "My name is Steele Austin."

The man was wearing red-framed glasses. He managed to both look over the top of the glasses and down at Steele while surveying him from head to toe. Then with a voice that sounded like he was swallowing his vowels and forcing a pseudo British accent, he offered Steele a limp and somewhat clammy hand. *"And so you are."*

Under the man's gaze Steele suddenly felt very small and insignificant. Steele glanced over at Bishop Powers. He was obviously enjoying the entire scene. "Steele, this is The Reverend Canon Doctor Niles Middleton Calhoun."

Steele nodded. "Are you a descendent of John Calhoun?"

The man continued to look down at Steele. "I believe you mean the Vice President that served with distinction under two Presidents of the United States."

Steele only nodded for fear that he might be subjected to a lengthy history lesson.

"Well, I certainly share the same Ulster Scot blood that flowed through the veins of the esteemed orator."

Steele couldn't let that one go. "I fear I'm not familiar with the term Ulster Scot."

"Of course you're not." The man's voice now sounded almost pathetic. "In the motherland that term is used to describe those of us of Scotch Irish descent." The man continued to study Steele. "May I inquire as to your ancestral blood line?"

Steele shrugged. "I think the most interesting thing is that both my grandmothers were Cherokee Indians."

"Yes. I see it." The man pulled a cigarette from a silver case that he had been carrying in his inside jacket pocket. He placed the cigarette in a long cigarette holder and lit it. He lifted his head toward the sky and blew the smoke into the air. His gaze fell back on Steele. "Didn't the Cherokee interbreed with the Negroes?"

Steele decided he was not going to suffer this egomaniac any further. "I only wish my ancestors could have been that fortunate."

For the first time the man gave Steele a slight smile. "Well played, Mister Austin." Then he looked over at Bishop Powers. "I like him."

"I knew you would. My house is next to Steele's. Let's go up, sit down, and have a morning beverage."

"Do you have bourbon?"

"I do."

"Powdered sugar?"

"If you're asking me if I have the ingredients for Mint Juleps, I've already marinated the mint and have it ready to put through the strainer."

Niles Calhoun started leading the way to the bishop's house. "You are a gentleman's gentleman."

Steele found the Mint Juleps a little too sweet for his taste. The three of them were seated in rocking chairs on the bishop's screened porch overlooking the beach. Niles Calhoun began a monologue that neither the bishop nor Steele dared to interrupt. "I just got back from London. I attended Mass at Saint Paul's Cathedral. It was heaven on earth. Then I went to All Saints Church on Margaret Street for evensong. It was simply glorious. The incense was so thick the altar seemed to be floating. I flew over on the Concorde but returned on the Queen Mary. I only agreed to the return by sea after I'd received assurance that proper worship services would be made available on the ship. Do either of you play bridge?"

"I don't. Do you, Steele?" Bishop Powers was lighting a cigarette.

"No. I never learned."

"What a shame. Duplicate bridge has been my primary avocation since my retirement. I have earned over one hundred and fifty master points. I've exceeded the sixteen hundred level."

"I'm sorry. I don't know what all that means, but it does sound impressive." Steele offered.

"My dear boy, what it means is that I can no longer compete against amateurs. I am restricted to the shark pool."

"May I ask you a personal question, Canon Calhoun?" Steele looked directly at him. "How long were you a priest?"

"Unless you've received some communication from my Diocesan that I don't know about, I believe I remain a priest in good standing."

"No, I didn't mean that. How long were you in the parish?"

"Thirty years to the day. Lest you need to inquire further, I need to tell you that I never served in the office of rector. I was delivered from that. I was always an associate. My final ten years were spent at the cathedral in Charleston. I was the cathedral canon."

"Did you enjoy it?

"For the most part, but I enjoy my retirement more. I have more time to devote to duplicate bridge, my friends, and my family. I do manage a couple of white tie balls a year and several black tie dinners. Of course the highlight for me is the Burns Night celebration of the Saint Andrew's Society in Charleston each year."

"Burns Night?" Steele dared to ask.

"You're not familiar...*of course*." Steele could hear Niles swallow. He took a long pause and then continued. "It was established in honor of the eighteenth century Scottish Poet John Burns." Niles continued to stare at Steele as he pulled the smoke from his cigarette deep into his lungs. He exhaled the smoke directly at Steele. "Since you are unfamiliar with the Burns Ball, I guess it goes without saying that you are equally ill-informed on the Saint Cecilia Society."

Steele glanced over at Bishop Powers, who simply shrugged his shoulders. "I know that Saint Cecilia is the patron saint of music." Steele offered apologetically.

"My dear boy. At least you have a start, but as a clergyman in the Episcopal Church, the mother church of this country, you simply must familiarize yourself with the history that the theological institutions fail to provide. The Saint Cecilia Society is absolutely the oldest and most exclusive society in this country. The ball is an extravagant affair and held annually in Charleston. Membership is open only to those that are blood descendents of the original members."

"When was it founded?"

Niles gave Steele an exasperated look. "It predates the foundation of this nation. The landed gentry that came to this country originated the society in 1766. Only the finest citizens were ever allowed to attend. It is the oldest music subscription society in America."

"Okay. Thanks for the education. I feel like I should have known all that already." Steele could feel himself shrink underneath the man's gaze. He desperately wanted to change the subject. He also wanted to know more about Niles' ministry. He smiled and asked bravely. "Were you ever tempted to be a rector?"

"It's fascinating that you should ask. I was asked to serve as the interim at my current parish, but to my regret, I declined."

"So you wish that you'd done it?"

"Only because our current interim has brought so much uncertainty to our little family. Temporary clergy are a lot less satisfactory than one that has made the commitment to stay. Needless to say, a permanent rector is more capable of knowing what actually needs to be done. The temporary ones just tinker with the liturgy and do little else."

Bishop Powers was lighting a fresh cigarette off the one he'd just finished. "Niles, Steele is on sabbatical. He's actually trying to decide if he wants to return to his parish or pursue another career."

For the first time, Calhoun looked at Steele with genuine concern on his face. "You poor boy. I can only tell you that I had a lovely time in my ministry. As I told you, God delivered me from the woes so many rectors are subjected to. I guess I would do it all again." He paused and put a new cigarette in his holder. He leaned his head up against the back of his rocker and began to gently rock. He held the cigarette holder in his teeth with a slight grin on his face.

Steele watched him. He thought for an instant he looked just like the photos of Franklin Delano Roosevelt he'd seen. He thought better of suggesting that Niles Middleton Calhoun looked like a Yankee President.

"The only thing I can suggest to you, Mister Austin, is that if you return, you'd better get used to living close to the poverty line. My first priorities are to pay my pledge to the cathedral and the various societies I hold membership in. After I subtract my meager living expenses I just do have enough left to maintain my membership in the Charleston Country Club. Mind you, some months it's a close call."

Steele smiled and nodded. Bishop Powers rolled his eyes.

chapter 28

SEAN EVANS OPENED the door to his new office. The walls were bare and freshly painted. The new furniture he'd ordered for his office had arrived. The furniture was arranged pretty much the way Bishop Petersen had it, with one notable exception. Sean did not order purple furniture. His experience with John North in New York had pretty well soured him on the color purple. He ordered that the carpet be replaced with a silver gray one. The heavy furniture was blue. The accent chairs were striped blue, red, and cream.

Sean placed his briefcase on top of the desk. He walked over to one of the wingback chairs sitting next to a large window overlooking the cathedral gardens. This would be his daily view for the next twenty years. He liked it.

"Bishop Evans, I presume." Canon Jim Vernon shut the door behind him and locked it. He walked up to Sean and took his face in his hands and kissed him with desperation. "God, I've been waiting for this moment," he uttered, breathless.

Sean patted him and pushed him away. "That's got to wait. We have a lot of work to do."

"Well, if you say so, but the way I feel right now, it wouldn't take but a few minutes. I locked the door."

Sean smiled. "I wouldn't be able to concentrate. I have so much on my mind. There's so much I need to tell you."

"Okay, Bishop. Business before pleasure."

"I told you as much as I felt like I could on the telephone. There's so much more we need to discuss."

"You got anything to write on in here?" Jim pulled out one of the drawers on Sean's desk. "Here's a white legal pad. Okay, shoot." He took a seat opposite Sean by the window.

"Were you able to get a current picture of that nutty woman?"

"I actually have three." Jim opened the manila folder he'd tossed on a side table when he walked into his office. "The rector sent them up. This one is from the photo directory the parish did." He handed Sean the photograph. "These are from a parish party. He said she liked getting in front of the camera."

Sean studied the photographs. "My God, just look at her. She looks like a Looney Tune. Just looking at her picture should have been enough to put an end to all of the crap they've put me through. Make sure all the security guards have a copy of these pictures just in case she does show up and try to disrupt the service."

"Was it pretty rough up there in New York?"

"I guess not. It was just a hassle I didn't need. It certainly took some of the air out of the joy I was feeling. Now I just want to get my consecration over with so I can get on with my job."

"About your consecration...we've run into a couple of snags."

Sean laid his head back against his chair and shut his eyes. "What is going on? Has Satan assigned one of his demons to me full time? Is none of this going to go smoothly?"

"The comptroller is giving me grief about some of the expenditures."

"Like what?"

"Well, the venue first. He says the diocese can't afford to rent the city auditorium. He insists that you do your service here at the cathedral. They can set up overflow seating in the chapel and the great hall with live video feeds."

"How many people will that accommodate?"

"He says two thousand. I personally went over with the sextons and set up chairs in the great hall. We allowed eighteen inches per person in the pews. Sean, they won't be able to seat more than eight hundred people. The clergy and convention delegates alone will require five hundred of those seats. I wish that were all, but he's having a hissy fit about hosting a reception after the ordination."

"You've got to be kidding me."

"I wish I were. He's really being a prick about everything. I told him that we'd just wait until you get here and then decide. In the meantime, I have the convention center holding the date. I also have the Hyatt ballroom across the street from the center reserved for a reception."

"When do we meet with him?"

"I think he's in his office now."

"Bring him down here."

The comptroller was a chunky little man just about as wide as he was tall. He was wearing one of the worst toupees Sean had ever seen in his life. He had to resist the urge to simply snatch it off his head and throw it in the trash. "Bishop Evans," he grinned, extending his hand. "I guess I can call you bishop. We've been so excited for you to arrive. I look forward to working with you."

Sean motioned for him to sit down. "How long have you been the comptroller for this diocese?"

"You will be the third bishop I've worked for."

"It's my understanding that the diocesan council passed a budget for the election, moving costs, and consecration of a new bishop."

"Yes sir. That's correct."

"Did the election process deplete that budget?"

"No. There's sufficient funds remaining to afford you a real nice service, but I need to be careful."

"Just one correction to begin. It won't be my service. The consecration of a new bishop is a diocesan event. It's a time for the entire diocese to celebrate. It begins a new chapter in their life. So you see, it's not about me."

He gave Sean a patronizing smile. "I stand corrected. I really appreciate the lesson."

"Now, how much have we expended so far?"

"Well, I haven't received all the invoices for your move yet, but as of this morning, I've paid out right at thirty thousand dollars on the search and election process. Your move and new furniture so far has cost me right at twelve thousand dollars. So that leaves me about eight thousand dollars for a service."

Jim began tapping his pen on the legal pad he was holding. Sean looked at him. Jim rolled his eyes. "So you're telling me that the council only budgeted sixty thousand dollars for a search, election, move and installation of a new bishop?"

"Well, I was thinking I could do it for sixty thousand dollars total. Maybe I could do it for less if the flowers for the Sunday services at the cathedral could be put up a day early."

"I notice that you keep using the pronoun—*I*. You do realize that it's not your money."

"Oh, I didn't mean to suggest that it was. "

"What did you mean?"

"Well, it's just that I'm responsible for writing the checks. I have to authorize all the expenditures."

"So you set the budget."

"No, the council sets the budget."

"That's correct. The council sets the budget and you simply issue the checks for authorized expenditures."

"Well, bishop, I've just always tried to be as frugal as possible with the money I was entrusted with."

"Correction. You're not entrusted with the money. The bishop and trustees of the diocese are the trustees. The council approves the budget. You write the checks as directed. Nothing more."

"Well, that's just not the way I've understood my job."

Sean studied him for a few minutes. He could tell he was not happy. He began to wonder if perhaps there wasn't more to his frugality than met the eye. The line between frugality and greed is a thin one. Sean decided he'd have a word with the auditors. "So let me ask you again. How much did the council authorize?"

"As I said I was hoping I...urh...we could do everything for sixty-thousand dollars."

"That wasn't my question. This is the last time I'm going to ask it. How much did the council authorize?"

The man shuffled in his seat. "They set aside two hundred thousand for everything. I just think that's too exorbitant."

Sean looked at Jim and winked. "Well, if it makes you feel any better, we're not going to need anything near that."

The man brightened. "Well, I'm certainly glad to hear that."

"I'll bet you are." Sean stood and offered his hand to him. He took it and they shook. "You've served the diocese a long time. I believe you are eligible to retire. I'm going to suggest that you do that soon after I'm ordained."

"But I don't want to retire."

Sean put his hand on his shoulder and looked him in the eye. "You have a choice. You can retire within sixty days of my ordination or I will fire you. You choose."

The man turned and walked out of the bishop's office, shutting the door behind him.

chapter 29

THE TRUCK STOP smelled of cigarettes, beer, grease and body odor. There were just a few diners at the counter. Henry speculated that they were the drivers of the big rigs parked around the building. The booths were all empty. Henry took a seat in one by the window. A waitress with a cigarette dangling from her mouth asked him what he wanted. "Just coffee to begin with."

Soon he saw Virginia enter. She spotted him immediately. He stood and extended his hand for her to shake. "You've lost weight, Virginia."

"Thank you. I actually now weigh exactly what I weighed on our wedding day. Do you remember?"

"I remember." He studied her critically. She was staring at him with anticipation. "Virginia, let me set some ground rules. I have no intention of walking down memory lane with you. I've come to hear about your so-called emergency. Then there's something I want to tell you."

"You're still angry with me."

"You want coffee, lady?" The waitress with yet another cigarette hanging out of her mouth was standing at the table.

"Could I suggest that you knock those ashes off your cigarette." Henry pointed at her cigarette.

"Sure, no problem." She then reached past Henry across the table and dropped the ashes in the ashtray next to him. "Now what do you want?"

"I'll have two poached eggs and dry wheat toast." Virginia ordered.

"I'll have the same. And could I ask you not to have a cigarette dangling from your mouth when you bring our food?"

The lady gave Henry a look that contained an unmistakable message. "Yes, *your royal highness.*"

"You are still angry, aren't you?" Virginia placed her hand on top of Henry's. He jerked his hand away.

"You're damn right I'm still angry. I've tried to put our marriage behind me but what you did still haunts me. You lied to me and then you betrayed me with other men. You humiliated me in the eyes of my family and friends. Those men you screwed were either laughing at me, feeling sorry for me, or thinking I must be the dumbest bastard in the world."

"Henry, if you could only forgive me."

"And then what?"

"You don't think you could ever forgive me enough to allow us to have another chance? Maybe for the sake of our daughters we could try again."

"Together? You actually think I could take you back? How could I ever touch you without wondering if one of your lovers had also touched you in the same place? How would I know whether or not you're lying to me? How would I ever be able to trust you again? Every time you left the house I'd be wondering whom you were going to meet. Do you think that I could actually make love to you without having one of the ghosts of your adulterous slime balls make an appearance in my head? How would I ever know if you were thinking about me or one of your man whores? I was listening to the radio on the way over here. They played one of the songs you always requested. I began to wonder whether you wanted to hear that song because it reminded you of one of your adulterers. I'd never know when you were listening to music just who you were thinking about. Virginia, you have no idea of the hurt and humiliation I live with since I divorced you. It would be unbearable if I were still married to you. Any husband that can stay married to a lying, cheating, whoring wife that has screwed around on him is a better man than me."

"Henry, I've told you a thousand times how sorry I am."

"Sometimes being sorry just won't fix it. The video of you and your lovers in my head just won't turn off. It runs day and night. Frankly, I don't know how you can live with yourself."

"Eggs and toast for the King and Queen." The waitress smarted as she sat their plates in front of them and poured them more coffee. "Look, no cigarette, Your Majesty."

"You do work for tips, don't you?" Henry barked.

"Yes, *Your Excellency*. That's how I afford that big black Mercedes parked out there in my reserved spot." She put a green sales receipt on the table. "You pay the cashier. I'll try to live without your tip. I'm sure my children can go without food one more day." With that she walked away.

"I don't think she likes you, Henry. Do you think it's safe to eat these eggs?"

Henry pushed his plate away. "What's this all about, Virginia? What's the emergency?"

"Henry, I just don't have any other place to turn. I need your help."

"How much do you need, Virginia?"

"How did you know I was going to ask you for assistance?"

"I know you, Virginia. Although I have to confess I'd expected this call long before now."

"I've sold most everything I own. I have nothing left and now my rent is due."

"Put away the violins. How much?"

"Well, my rent is due and I don't have it."

"How much?" Henry could not hide the irritation in his voice.

"I need six hundred dollars."

"Six hundred dollars. Where the hell are you living?"

"I just have a two room duplex over near the Mill Village."

"Good God, Virginia. I gave you a good settlement." Tears started running down Virginia's face. Henry wiped the sweat off his mouth with his napkin and tossed it on the table. "What about the next month's rent?"

"I guess I'm going to have to get a job."

"You guess? That thought didn't cross your mind before now? You have a possibility?"

"No; I thought I might go to the bank. Maybe I could get a job there."

"When's the last time you had a drink or smoked a joint?"

"I had a brief relapse about a month ago but I've been sober since."

"Gee, a whole month."

"Henry, it's hard."

"What about that slut Alicia? Are you still hanging out with her?"

"No. My sponsors and my groups convinced me she was a bad influence."

"Virginia, I want you to do more to make amends with our daughters."

"I'm trying, Henry. I'd hoped I could have them come spend weekends with me, but my place is so small there's hardly enough room for me."

"I'll tell you what I'm going to do, Virginia. Do you remember the little rental house I bought over on the Savannah Highway?"

"I do. It's cute. I remember at the time thinking it was awfully cute."

"Virginia, it's vacant right now. I'm going to let you live in it rent-free."

"Oh, Henry, thank you. Thank you so much."

"Don't thank me just yet. I have conditions."

"That's the answer to my prayer. It has two bedrooms. I can ask the girls to come spend the night with me. We can become close again."

"That's part of the condition. I'm not doing this for you, Virginia. I'm doing this for the girls. I want them to have a decent place to go when they come visit you."

"Thank you, Henry. I mean it. Thank you."

"Well, in spite of your multiple failings as a wife, you were a good mother. I want my daughters to have a positive relationship with their mother. It's essential to their development or they'll end up being even more screwed up than you are."

"That hurts." She whimpered.

"I told you. No violins. You chose this. You have no one to blame but yourself. I was good to you, Virginia. My problem is that I was too good to you. I blame myself for that. I trusted you. I believed in you. I believed that our marriage vows were just as sacred to you as they were to me. You lied to me and you lied to God. I'm guilty of giving you too much freedom and far too much pampering. So now put your big girl panties on and deal with the consequences of the decisions you made."

"What did you want to tell me?"

"What I have to tell you also comes with conditions. I've met somebody, Virginia."

"I thought as much."

"How do you know?"

"I saw her with the girls downtown. They didn't see me, but I saw them. She's mighty pretty."

"Yes. She's beautiful. I love her and she loves me. The girls are crazy about her."

"I know."

"Virginia, if all goes well, I plan on asking her to marry me."

"Oh." More tears welled up in Virginia's eyes. "I see."

Henry broke the silence that had developed between them. "The house comes with the condition that you don't do or say anything to screw up my marriage to Delilah."

"Delilah? Is that her name? Like in the Bible?"

"Yes. Do you agree to my conditions?"

"I do."

"Now Virginia, you take note of this and you emblazon it across your forehead. You fall off the wagon, go back to your slutty ways, fail to work on a relationship with our daughters, or do anything to screw up my marriage…"

"I know. I know," she interrupted.

Henry pointed his finger at her. "If I get wind that you've violated one of those conditions I will throw your ass out of that house and into the alley before you even know what has happened. Do I make myself clear?"

Virginia nodded, wiping the tears from her cheeks. Henry reached into his jacket pocket and handed her a set of keys. These are to the house. You can move in at any time, but you'll pay your own utilities. You're also responsible for your own move."

"Thank you, Henry. I can do that. I'm going to get a job. My friends in my new church will help me move. Did I tell you I have a new church?"

"That's fine, Virginia. See if you can't pay attention to what they're teaching."

"Henry, please."

Henry stood and picked up the check. "Do you remember Thackston Willoughby?"

"The attorney? Sure I do. I always thought he liked me."

"You just can't get over yourself, can you? Does every person in the world have to approve of you? Guess what? They don't and every man is not hot to lay you." Henry looked disgusted. "All right then. Thackston is looking for a receptionist. He asked me if I knew anyone I could recommend. I told him about you. He said to come see him. If you want it, the job is yours."

Virginia jumped up from the booth and threw her arms out to hug Henry. He stopped her. "Don't even think about it. Just remember that if you don't live up to your end of the bargain you can find yourself a shopping cart. And Virginia, I won't care."

Henry reached for his money clip. He pulled out a fifty-dollar bill and threw it on the table. "Virginia, that's not for you. That's for the waitress. At least she gave me something to smile about today." He remained standing staring at Virginia. She grew uncomfortable under his gaze and sat back down. "I never really knew you, did I, Virginia? You had a secret life that I knew nothing about. I was literally married to a stranger. But Virginia, I know you now. Frankly, I don't like you." Henry then turned and left the restaurant.

Virginia remained in the booth in order to finish her coffee. When she saw Henry's Mercedes exit the parking lot she picked up the fifty-dollar bill and left.

chapter 30

"I LIKE WHAT you've done with the office." Bishop Petersen stood in the middle of what was his domain for over fifteen years.

"Please, come sit by the window. My hunch is that you've spent a lot of time in this spot." Sean Evans poured Bishop Petersen a cup of tea. "Your secretary told me you were now a tea man."

"I had my heart attack right here on this spot. It was a real wake-up call for me."

"That's what I understand."

"Are you going to keep her?"

"Who?" Sean asked.

Rufus nodded toward the secretary's office. "Her."

"I was thinking about it. She's impressed me with her efficiency."

"You know she has a mouth on her."

"I've already been corrected on several things. She's also been quite generous with her counsel."

Rufus chuckled, "Oh, you don't understand. That's not counsel. In her mind those are ultimatums. I probably should have fired her."

"Why didn't you?"

He looked down at the floor. Sean detected a note of sadness. "I guess I grew fond of her. I hope you'll give her a chance."

"That's my intention."

"I don't want to get in your business. In a few days you'll be the ordained bishop of this diocese. I'll be in Florida. My only sister lives on the gulf coast. I'm going to go live near her. In your twilight years it's best to be near family."

"You'll be at my consecration, won't you?"

"I wouldn't miss it." Rufus swallowed some of the tea in his cup. "I understand that you're retiring the comptroller."

"I may have made a rash decision on that one, but he just rubbed me wrong within minutes of meeting him. I just don't think I can work with him."

"No, you made the right decision. I really should have done that myself. He thought the diocesan treasury was his own."

"Did you ever suspect any malfeasance?"

"No, I think he's just cheap."

"Cheap and greed are two sides of the same coin. I need you to know that I'm going to have someone take a forensic look at the books."

"I could be wrong, but I don't think you'll find anything. I guess if I were in your situation, I'd do the same thing."

"I'll let you know if we find anything."

"Thanks. Like I said, I don't want to get in your business, but I brought you this. He handed Sean a thick brown envelope. You can open this or you can shred it. It's up to you. I just took the liberty of giving you my evaluation of each of the clergy in the diocese and their congregations."

"Gosh, Bishop, this is a lot of work. Thanks."

"Well, over the past few weeks I haven't had much to do but pack boxes and say my *goodbyes*. You're going to see that there are clergy that I think are doing excellent work. Then there are others that I think should move on. You'll just have to see if you agree."

"I plan to take my time. I not only want to visit the congregations on Sundays, but I hope to go out during the week and spend a day or two with each of the rectors."

"I hope you're able to do that. Sometimes I felt like a prisoner in this office."

"Why do I get the feeling that you have something else you want to share with me?"

"Am I that obvious?"

"Let's just say I can tell when a person needs to unburden himself."

"How much do you know about First Church in Falls City?"

"I know it's the largest in the diocese. I also know they have a pretty controversial rector."

Rufus sat forward in his chair. "Let's talk about Steele Austin. Yes, he's been controversial, but he's doing some impressive work. He's grown the parish, added services, quadrupled the budget and still had time to start several major service ministries to the poor in the community."

"Wow. That's really impressive. I understand that his wife is quite the looker."

"She's really beautiful." Rufus got a twinkle in his eye. "You know, I've always thought that you could measure the holiness of a priest by the beauty of his wife." Rufus chuckled. "If I'm right about that, then a lot of our priests are in trouble."

"I sure hope you're wrong about that particular measuring stick of holiness. I understand that a group went after both him and his wife."

"That's right. A small group up there tried to destroy him. They were trying to get me to work with them to toss him out. They almost sucked me in."

"But you had a change of heart."

"No, I had a change of facts. They were manufacturing everything they were accusing him of doing. Mind you, he's not perfect and he's done some things in ways you or I would not have done them."

"What about the group?"

"I removed them. I understand they're now going to the Presbyterian Church."

"I admire you for doing that."

The sad look returned to Rufus' face. "I should have done it sooner. I should have done the same thing for a dozen others."

"I understand Father Austin is on a sabbatical."

"That's correct. I fear he may not return. If he doesn't it will be a real loss not only to First Church but to this diocese."

"Do you think I should try to contact him?"

"I don't know. You're closer to his age. You young priests have a different way of doing things than my generation. I'm hoping that you'll be able to speak his language. I'm even hoping the two of you will be friends."

"Thanks, Bishop. If he comes back I'll certainly do my part."

"Well, I'd better go. You have a lot to do. Are the plans for your consecration moving along?"

"I think everything is pretty well set. You have my numbers. Call me if I can do anything for you."

Rufus Petersen stood and took one last long look around what was once his office. "I guess I'd better be on my way. It's a strange feeling being put out to pasture."

Sean stood and opened his arms to hug him. The two men embraced. "Bishop, can I ask you to do one thing for me before you leave?"

"Certainly. Anything you want."

"I'd like your blessing." Then Sean knelt before the Bishop. The Right Reverend Rufus Petersen then gave his very last blessing in the office he'd so cherished. With a quivering voice, shaking hands and eyes blinded by tears he blessed the man who would be the next bishop of the Diocese of Savannah.

⚜

chapter 31

THE PEOPLE AT St. Andrew's Presbyterian Church were first informed that things just might be amiss when they received a letter from the president of the session. It was signed by every member of the session. The letter was only one page long. It stated simply that the senior pastor had been placed on an indefinite leave of absence. For privacy reasons, the session was unable to reveal the exact reasons for the leave. The letter continued to recite the many strengths of the parish. It reassured the congregation that each member of the session was completely committed to the parish and the ministry of the church. The congregation was assured that the associate clergy and staff would continue to maintain the worship schedule and the many ministries of the parish. The letter then Thanked the members of the congregation for their commitment. They asked the membership to pray for the senior pastor and his wife and children during a period of uncertainty. They closed by asking that the members also pray for the session. Their daily prayer was that the Lord's will be done.

It did little to alleviate the anxiety and the gossip that spread through the congregation and beyond. The speculation was further fueled when the local and state newspapers each carried stories reporting that the senior pastor at St. Andrew's Church had been placed on indefinite leave by the session. The newspapers included his photo and a history of the parish. They reported that telephone calls to the session leaders and the presbytery in Savannah had not been returned.

"I heard he had a girlfriend."

"No, I heard he was misappropriating money."

"That can't be true. He was such a wonderful preacher. I think he's being set up. You know that there were a few that were opposed to him."

"That may be true, but I know that there was conflict between some of the session leaders and him."

"No, you all have it wrong. It's his wife. I have it on good authority that she's left him."

"I hate to be the one to correct all of you, but I was at the Winn-Dixie this morning and two of the members told me that one of his children is on drugs. It's all just too much for him to handle so the session granted him leave."

"My brother-in-law is on the session and I asked him if the leave was forced or requested. The only thing I could get out of him was that it was forced."

"Well then, that brings us back to sex or money. He was either having an affair and got caught or he was using church funds for inappropriate purposes."

That conversation or one much like it was repeated wherever people gathered. In restaurants, at cocktail parties, stores, and around water coolers in offices and factories throughout the city, those who were certain pronounced their findings.

Harlan McMurray, Ned Boone, Judith and Elmer Idle sat at a sidewalk table at *Cup of Joes* on Main Street. One passerby from St. Andrew's spotted them. "Harlan, aren't these folks new members of St. Andrew's?"

"Yes, they are."

"Please let me apologize for all the unrest in our parish right now. We have a wonderful congregation. I've put my full faith in the session. I just know that they'll be able to do what's best for us. Please stay with us. You'll see. You made the right decision. We have a wonderful congregation. Pastors come and go but we'll still be here."

"What do you know, Harlan?" Judith asked, wide-eyed.

"I've never seen anything like it. The session members are all tight lipped. I can't even get anything out of my brother-in-law. Believe me I've tried, but no one is saying anything."

"Where's the preacher now?" Ned asked nonchalantly.

"I suppose he's over at his house."

"Is he saying anything?"

"The only thing I could get out of my brother-in-law is that he's saying he's innocent. He didn't do whatever they've accused him of."

Elmer's curiosity was getting to him. "So he is accused of doing something. Which is it, sex or money?"

"I wish I could tell you." Harlan took a drink of his coffee. "I simply don't know. I have to confess that I didn't like the man and I wanted him to leave, but this has really caught me off guard."

"You just never know the secrets some folks are living with." Ned assured him.

"Did your detective find anything?" Harlan questioned. "Remember Ned, you told us that he did."

Ned nodded. "He found something. Like I said before, I think it's best that the information come out through other channels. I don't want it to come from me or any of you." Ned looked at Harlan. "Did they do the computer audit?"

"Yes, sir. My brother-in-law did thank me for that tip. He didn't say any more than that."

"So whatever they found they most likely found on the computer." Elmer looked at Ned. "Would that be the way they could discover what your detective discovered, Ned?"

Ned pursed his lips. "That would be one of the ways. That's why I suggested you talk to the auditors."

"What is the next step, Harlan?"

"I honestly don't know. The session will continue to investigate and then I guess they'll make the decision as to whether or not to fire him or bring him back."

"Do you think they'll let him come back?"

"Either way, they'll have to do a lot of explaining."

One week later Ned Boone was sitting at the desk in his home study. His maid brought him his mail on a silver tray. He thumbed through it. His eye fell on a letter from St. Andrew's Presbyterian Church. It was addressed to the membership.

It is with a heavy heart that we are forced to announce the dismissal of our senior minister. We are unable to provide you with the details of this deci-

sion but assure you that it is in his best interest and that of his family that we not do so. The presbytery is requiring him to seek psychological counseling. As to his future in the ministry, we are unable to say. We ask you to continue to pray for him and his family. We are in the process of putting together a search committee to seek the services of a new senior pastor. The letter was signed by all the members of the session.

A large smile spread across Ned's face. He picked up his desk telephone and called Harlan McMurray. "Have you read your letter?"

"My brother-in-law called me before breakfast this morning to let me know that it was coming."

"Did he tell you what they found?"

"Yes, but he swore me to secrecy."

"I understand." Ned was determined to hear the accusation for himself. "Harlan, remember my detective already told me what he found. I'm the one that suggested the audit of his computer."

"I know that, but the nature of this is so repulsive I promised him I wouldn't repeat it. I've not even told my own wife and that's his sister."

"Harlan, I already know something. I'd just like to know if what they found matches that. If not, you may need to tell the session to keep looking."

"Well, in that case I suppose I should tell you." Harlan whispered into the telephone. "Ned, they found pornographic pictures of underage teenage boys on his computer. He'd also visited teen boy sex websites."

Another smile spread across Ned's face. "That conforms with what my detective told me."

"Ned, the session doesn't want this to get out. I don't either."

"There's no need. He's gone now. Seems to me he's someone else's problem."

Ned hung up the receiver, then immediately picked it up and dialed another number. "I'll meet you there in ten minutes." He hung up the telephone and opened his desk drawer. He took out a thick white envelope. He walked out of his house and down the street to a little park. A young man was waiting for him on the park bench. He sat down next to him and discreetly handed him the envelope. "This is what we agreed on, plus a bonus."

The young man took the envelope. "Do you have another job for me?"

"Not just yet, but I have your number."

The young man left. Ned decided to sit on the bench and enjoy the warm sun on his face. It was such a beautiful day.

⚜

chapter 32

"LET'S TREAT OURSELVES to a nice lunch." Bishop Powers drove Steele up the coast to Murrells Inlet. It's a quaint little village of restaurants and shops along the coastal marsh. The little community is just a few miles north of Pawleys Island. The tidal creeks and estuaries that wind their way along what is known as the South Carolina Low Country provide a constant supply of fish, shrimp and crab. The low country recipes have been handed down from generation to generation. Ever loyal to southern tradition, succeeding generations are hesitant to amend generational recipes in the slightest. Most low country chefs pride themselves on not doing any fancy cooking. They prefer local foods prepared with local family recipes.

Bishop Powers parked in the tiny parking lot outside a colorful little restaurant painted pink and purple. Once inside, they settled into a window table overlooking the marsh. The Atlantic Ocean was visible just beyond the marsh. The dark knotty pine on all the walls automatically drew one's eyes to the windows. "The month has gone fast."

"You can say that again. I hate to leave. This has really been wonderful. Thanks for arranging this for us. And thanks for all the talks."

The bishop took a long hard look at Steele. "Well, I can say you look a lot better than you did thirty days ago. You've gotten some sun so at least your ancestors will be able to recognize you. You've put on a little weight, but you're still too thin."

"Is that even possible? I didn't think you could be too rich or too thin."

"You'd look better with a few more pounds. I have a feeling that Randi will make sure that happens."

"What can I get you, gentlemen?" A waitress in a pink dress with a white lace apron over it was standing at their table.

"What do you recommend?"

"We have a lunch special." She smiled. "But it's also our dinner special."

"Tell us about it."

Just then a busboy brought a basket of what Steele thought was hush puppies to the table. "What are these?" He asked.

"Those. Those are corndodgers."

"What are corndodgers?"

"They're sort of a fried cornmeal cake."

"So they're the same as hush puppies."

"No." She smiled. "These are better."

"You were telling us about your specials."

"We'll start you off with some she crab soup in a crusty bread bowl."

"That should be enough." Steele interrupted.

"Shoot, no! That's just the start. You also get a pimento cheese and crab bake with that. Don't worry. It comes in a small bowl."

"Well, that's sounds good." Steele took one of the corndodgers. "I'll have that."

"Don't you want the rest?"

Steele shot the bishop a look. "There's more?"

"Yes, then I'll bring you our seafood platter."

"What's on that?"

"Today, it has flounder, a lump crab cake, oysters, shrimp and scallops with a bowl of stone ground grits on the side."

"We'll both have that." Bishop Powers ordered.

"Can I have mine grilled?" Steele inquired.

"Where are you from?"

"Falls City, Georgia."

"Well, you should know better. This is the low country. We like our food fried."

"Boy, it's a good thing I'm leaving tomorrow. This cooking may be putting some weight on me, but I'm beginning to wonder about my arteries."

Bishop Powers laughed. "I think you'll be okay. Where are you all going from here?"

"Amanda's godparents live in Los Angeles. We're catching a plane tomorrow to go see them. Travis is excited about going to Disneyland again."

"Mickey Mouse."

"Yeah, but he's more fascinated with Winnie the Pooh. Anyway, it'll be a good time. It will be great to see our friends again."

"Steele, where are you in your thinking?"

"Randi and I have had a lot of time to talk. I think at this point we're leaning toward moving back to Oklahoma."

"It'll be nice to have you back in the diocese. Do you want me to put your name in some parishes? I have a couple of vacancies right now."

"I don't think so. I have a friend that has real estate offices in Tulsa and Oklahoma City. I'm thinking that I'm going to call her."

"I have to tell you that I'm disappointed."

"I thought you would be."

"What was the determining factor in your decision?"

"Bishop, I just don't belong. I don't fit. Randi doesn't fit."

"In what way?"

"I think I'm just too progressive for them. Before I got there they had a nice exclusive parish. It was the epicenter of Falls City Society. It was where young lawyers could fulfill their community service obligations by serving on the vestry. If you wanted to run for political office you needed to be a member of First Church. The registry of all the exclusive clubs was taken directly from the membership directory. Bishop, it was the place to be married. The primary reason people showed up on Sunday was to see and be seen."

"You had a larger vision."

"Here are your specials, gentlemen." The waitress and busboy began placing multiple plates on the table in front of the bishop and Steele.

"We need a bigger table." Steele observed. "There's no way I can eat all of this."

"Well, do what you can do. Steele, have you considered that just perhaps the problem is not the priesthood but the place?"

"I hadn't thought about it like that."

"As a favor to me and to yourself before you hang up your collar, could I ask you to think about two things?"

"Sure."

"What would your ministry look like if you were in a parish that shared your vision?"

"It would be easier."

"Okay. Let me give you one more thing to consider. How would your ministry at First Church be different if you gave them the choice of living into your vision? If they choose not to, wouldn't that be a clear sign that maybe you should seek another parish that's more compatible?

"I don't think they will."

"Don't you owe it to yourself and to them to find out before you just walk away?"

Steele nodded, but he knew he'd have to discuss it with Randi.

❦

chapter 33

SEAN AND JIM woke up in each other's arms. Their naked bodies were entangled. "I like your new digs." Jim yawned.

"Thanks." Sean wiped his eyes.

"Is this a new bed?"

"Just the mattress. Do you like it?"

"I do." Sean patted it. "Nice and firm like you."

"Jim, I think we need to talk."

"That sounds serious."

"You know that I love you."

"And I love you. So what's up?"

Sean sat up in the bed so that he could look at Jim. "I really enjoyed last night."

Jim smiled. "So did I. Twice and then again around four this morning if I remember correctly."

Sean felt himself blush. "I just think we're going to have to really be careful."

"I know, but don't you think it would be okay if I moved in here with you?"

"No. I just don't think that would be wise. We can't afford to have even the slightest suspicion raised about our working relationship."

"I know that, but…"

"No *buts*, Jim. I'm going to be the bishop of a very conservative diocese. The only way I can be effective in this diocese is if they perceive me as a celibate, single, heterosexual priest. That's the way I left it with that shrink in New York and that's the way the larger Church has to see me."

"Don't you think we can do something to change the thinking of the diocese? I know for a fact that we have half a dozen gay priests in this diocese. A couple of them are married. None of them can afford to be out of the closet. I just think we might be able to educate the folks and make some changes."

"That's certainly my hope, but Jim, if I am outed my ministry is over. This diocese will simply not accept an openly gay bishop. I hope we can make some progress, but I don't want my episcopate defined by gay and lesbian issues."

Just then the telephone rang. Sean answered it. "This is Sean Evans."

"Congratulations, Bishop."

"Well, thank you. Who is this?"

"Let's just say I'm a friend."

"Do I know you?"

"We had an evening in Atlanta. Shucks, I thought you'd never forget me."

Sean was getting nervous but felt like he needed to hear what this caller wanted. "I'm sorry. Perhaps if you gave me your name."

"I noticed the newspaper reported you as unmarried. Don't you think the headline should have said something about the Diocese of Savannah electing a gay bishop?"

"What makes you think I'm gay? I am a single priest that's taken vows of celibacy.

"Good one, Sean. I have to confess it's nice to finally have a name to go with the face and all the other parts. That's not the name you gave me that unforgettable night in Atlanta. Shame. Shame, naughty boy."

Sean signaled for Jim to go into the living room and pick up the extension. "I beg your pardon."

"I think I do remember some begging."

"Why should I believe anything you have to say?"

The man laughed. "Sean…Sean…Sean."

"I think this conversation is over." Sean started to hang up the telephone.

"You have a brown birth mark on your right butt cheek. I found it interesting. It's shaped like the state of Utah. I really don't think the Mormons would approve of the things you do with a mark shaped like their state."

"What do you want?"

"I want to know what you're going to do for us."

"By us?"

"Your gay brothers and sisters."

"I plan to work for full acceptance."

"Right answer."

"Is there anything else?"

"Yes, I'll be watching you."

"What?"

"Let's just say if you don't use your newly acquired position of influence to work on our behalf, I will be forced to blow your cover."

Sean felt his heart pounding. "Let's just say that what you say about me is true and I'm not saying that it is. Have you considered the consequences?"

"What consequences?"

"If you do what you are threatening to do, then there will be a trial and I'll be removed. I won't be able to do anything for the gay community. In fact, it will do a lot of damage. The bishop they choose to replace me could be a real homophobe. Is that what you want?" The man was silent. "Are you still there?"

"I was just thinking. I guess I'm going to have to trust you to do what you say you're going to do."

"So I guess I've heard the last of you."

"Oh, no. I plan to keep in touch. In fact, several of us are coming to your consecration. We'll be holding a small demonstration outside the auditorium. You won't mind having a contingent of like-minded people carrying some rainbow flags and signs, will you? It'll be a nice way to welcome your guests."

"I really wish you wouldn't do that."

"Too late. I'll be talking to you, Bishop. Love for all." Then he hung up the telephone.

Sean sat down on the side of the bed. Jim came back in and knelt down on the floor in front of him. "Well, I don't guess we planned on anything like that, but don't worry about it. I think I know a good way to handle them."

"How? God, Jim, the last thing I need is to have my consecration turned into a Pride Parade."

"Leave it to me. I know exactly what to do. I don't want you to worry about it."

"Okay. I'll leave this one to you."

Jim looked up into Sean's eyes. "Now I know just how I can take your mind off all this." He then stood and pushed Sean back onto the bed.

⚜

chapter 34

VIRGINIA MUDD WASTED no time moving into her new house. Several of the people in her support group at the church helped her move. Her minister came as well. When they had everything in the house and most all the boxes were unpacked, he asked everyone to gather in the living room. They all joined hands. "Our Heavenly Father, we remember that the blessed family was homeless." Several in the room began praying with him. There were, *Yes, Lord,* and several muttered, *Jesus, oh sweet Jesus.* "Just as they had no place to lay their heads the night our Savior was born so our sister, Virginia, was wandering through the desert. But Lord, You in your providence have given this wonderful house into her hands." His voice rose in volume. "Let it be for her more than a house. Let it be a home for her and her precious daughters." His voice grew into a shout and those present were worked into even a greater fervor. "Let it be her home until she makes her entrance into that heavenly city. Let it be her home until she walks through those gates of pearl. Let it be her home until she walks those streets of gold. Let it be her home when she opens that door covered with diamonds and rubies and walks into the mansion of many rooms prepared for her. Thank you, Jesus. Thank you, Jesus. Amen and amen." His *amen's* were echoed by even more from those in the circle. Then there were hugs and pats on the back all around. Another group of ladies came into the house from the church. They were carrying baskets filled with food and beverages.

That evening Virginia sat in the living room of her new home. She was grateful to Henry for allowing her to live here. Maybe for the first time she was truly grateful to him for something he'd done for her. She thought back over her life with him. Maybe she never had loved him. She loved the lifestyle he provided for her. She loved the idea of being married to him. It was time for honesty. She needed to accept that she'd never been in love with him. The only man she had really been in love with was Jacque. Henry had been good to her in their marriage. He was an excellent husband. She just didn't love him. Oh, maybe she loved him as a brother, but Jacque...Virginia felt her loneliness for him return.

Just then there was a knock at her door. "Virginia, it's Alicia."

Virginia sat paralyzed in her chair.

"Virginia, I know you're in there. I can see you. Open the door."

Virginia didn't move. She knew she couldn't. She must not.

"I have goodies. I brought enough wine to wash away all our troubles." The fun that she and Alicia used to have together flashed before her.

"Virginia. There's more. I brought chocolate. You're going to want the chocolate. You'll need the chocolate."

Virginia stood and walked to the door. "Alicia..."

"There you are. I heard that you had moved. Open the door."

Virginia put her hand on the knob and started to turn it. She hesitated. "Alicia, I can't."

"What do you mean you can't?"

"Alicia, I've been clean for some time now. I'm in a twelve-step program. I'm giving all that stuff up."

"Oh Virginia, that's ridiculous. A little won't hurt you. The only difference between a drunk and an alcoholic is that a drunk doesn't have to go to those damn meetings. Let's just get drunk and celebrate your new house."

"Go away, Alicia. I can't see you ever again. Please. Please go away."

"Well that's a crappy way to treat your best friend." Alicia kicked Virginia's door with her foot.

Virginia stood quietly by the door until she heard Alicia's car drive away. She opened the door. There on her front porch were two bottles of wine. Virginia picked them up and carried them to the kitchen. She opened both of them. Then she poured the contents of each down the drain. That night Virginia Mudd slept better than she had in months. The next day she dressed in one of her prettiest dresses and drove to the law offices of Thackston Willoughby.

"Virginia, it's so nice to see you again."

"And it's nice to see you, Thackston."

"I was so sorry to hear about you and Henry. Are you all right?"

"I fear I'm in need of employment."

"That's what I understand. Can you start tomorrow? Let's say nine o'clock."

Thackston extended his hand to her. She cupped his hand in both of hers and then stroked it before she released it. She looked deep into his eyes and smiled. "How can I ever thank you?"

He stared back at her and smiled. "I had a light breakfast. I could use a little more to eat. Would you care to join me?"

"Mister Willoughby, do you think that would be appropriate? After all, I'm now your employee."

He took her hand and squeezed it. "I won't tell anyone if you don't."

As he helped Virginia Mudd into his brand new Jaguar, she gave her handsome new employer a sensual smile. She lifted her dress up well past her knees as she arranged herself on the seat. She could tell from the look of appreciation on his face he liked what he saw. Virginia felt just like a schoolgirl once again.

∞

chapter 35

"DEE, EVERYTHING LOOKS absolutely beautiful." Henry walked up behind her and put both of his arms around her waist. "You look beautiful and you smell so good."

"Thank you. You look pretty handsome yourself."

"Are you nervous?"

"Just a little. I'm excited to meet all your friends. I just don't want to do anything to embarrass you."

"There's no way that you can do that, but let me make one little correction. Not all the people you're going to meet this afternoon are my friends. I don't even like some of these snobs."

"Then why did you invite them?"

"Because I don't want them to be in a position to give you a hard time. I'm sorry. It's just the way things work in this town."

Delilah turned and put her hands on his chest. "I trust you. I just want everything to go well."

"Are the girls dressed?"

"Wait until you see them. Shady is helping them put on the finishing touches. We went to what seemed like a dozen stores before they each could find a dress they wanted to wear. They're very excited about hosting this party."

Just then the girls entered the dining room. Shady stood behind then with a big grin on her face. She was so proud. "Oh my gosh, Shady, who are these lovely creatures?"

"Oh, Daddy." They cooed.

Henry signaled for them to make a turn for him. They each obliged. "Shady, lock these girls in their rooms. I don't want them exposed to any young fellows that might show up. They'll try to run off with my beautiful daughters."

"Daddy, stop. Do you like our dresses?"

"Between you and Dee, I've never seen three more beautiful women in my life." The girls ran to Henry and hugged him. Then to his satisfaction, they hugged Dee.

"Daddy, what do you think of the food? Dee let us help her choose the menu."

Henry looked at all the silver trays strategically placed on the dining room table. They were stacked high with hors d'oeuvres. "Everything is perfect." Then Henry's eyes fell on a silver tray stacked with little square sandwiches. "What are these?"

"They're peanut butter and jelly sandwiches. That was our idea, Daddy. Don't you think they look good? Delilah suggested that we trim the crust off the bread and cut them into little squares. Wasn't that a good idea?"

"Yes, it was. I'm proud of all of you."

"Shady and I have just a few more things to set out," Delilah turned toward the kitchen.

"We want to help." The girls shouted in unison and chased after her into the kitchen.

"Come on." Delilah took their hands. "We can always use more help."

Henry walked into the living room where one of the bars had been set up. He'd hired a couple of the bartenders from The Magnolia Club for the party. "Samuel, how about a shot of liquid courage before these vultures all descend on us?"

"Yes suh, Misturh Henry. It looks to me like you got the entire club membership coming over here. Yes suh, it shore do."

Henry took his drink and stood at the window looking out on the front lawn. The valets were all in place. He knew that valet parking for his guests was a necessity. He reviewed the list in his mind. The Stone Clemons, Chief Sparks and his wife, the Howard Dexters, the Gordon Smthyes, Almeda and Horace Drummond, Mother Graystone, the parish deacon and most all the vestry. He didn't invite Gary Hendricks or Tom Barnhardt. He couldn't stand those two snakes. Then he'd invited the heads of all the proper clubs and societies in the city. It would literally be a gathering of who's who in Falls City. It was imperative that they all approve of the woman that he'd fallen in love with. The feel of arms around his waist interrupted his thoughts. "I'm sorry about the peanut butter and jelly sandwiches. It's just that they really wanted to have them as a part of our offerings. I just didn't have the heart to say no."

He turned and gathered her in his arms. "Damn, you're so beautiful. I just can't believe you've fallen in love with an ugly bloke like me."

"When is the last time you looked in a mirror? I'm the lucky one."

"He kissed her gently so as not to smear her lipstick. The sandwiches are fine. Thanks for making my girls feel a part of this."

Just then the doorbell rang. "I want you to stand with me at the door. I want to introduce you to all the guests as they arrive."

True to their reputation to always be the first to arrive and therefore the first at the food were Howard and Martha Dexter. "Howard... Martha. I'm so glad you could come. This is my friend, Delilah."

Martha looked Delilah up and down from head to toe. "Henry's forgotten that we've already met. But it is so nice to see you again."

Soon the house was filled with conversation. Mary Alice Smythe asked Almeda, "Are you going to the consecration of the new bishop?"

"Yes, we'll be there. The new bishop has been so considerate as to ask Horace to assist with the communion at the altar. It's a tremendous honor. We're looking forward to it. I'm actually trying to get Horace to go up a couple of days early. We could get a hotel and have some time in Savannah. I do love that city and we haven't been there for pleasure in some time."

"I think there's going to be quite a contingent from First Church. It seems like everyone I talk to is planning to attend."

"It will be a happy occasion."

Mary Alice put her hand on Almeda's arm. "I just wish it was Horace that we were ordaining."

Almeda forced a smile. "Frankly, I think he's relieved that it's not. I know that I'm relieved. I fear that if he were the bishop I'd never get to see him."

"What do you think of Delilah?"

"She appears to me to be perfectly lovely."

"Henry has been put through so much. He's been so humiliated. I just don't understand what gets into some women. Why on earth would any wife want to so disrespect her husband?"

Almeda felt the need to change the discussion. "Have you noticed the way Henry's girls just hang on her? They appear to be so fond of her."

"It appears to be that way to me."

"What are you all talking about?" Martha Dexter asked, spraying food out of her mouth.

"Martha, please don't talk with your mouth full." Mary Alice scolded.

She immediately covered her mouth with her hand. "We've been through this, Mary Alice. I have this horrible overbite. I just can't help it."

"Yes, you can. Swallow and then talk."

Martha flushed with embarrassment. She swallowed the food in her mouth. "Okay now, what are you talking about?"

"We were just discussing Henry's special friend."

"My Howard says that he's in love."

"How does Howard know that?"

"He says he knows when a man is in love. Henry has all the signs."

"Well, that may be." Almeda glanced over at Delilah. "She is lovely, isn't she?"

Mary Alice and Martha followed her gaze. Delilah was deep in conversation with the President of the Women's Club. "It looks like she has her approval."

Almeda grimaced. "If she has that old bat's approval, then she's in."

"Look at Delilah now." Mary Alice smiled. They all glanced toward her. One of Henry's daughters had walked up and put her arm around Delilah's waist.

Almeda straightened to her full height. "Henry has chosen well. Those girls need a woman in this house. Let's find him and let him know that very thing. You know men. They don't always know what's good for them. Come on ladies, let's find him."

They scanned the rooms for Henry. They finally spotted him in a far corner of the great room. He was standing in a corner talking to Chief Sparks and Stone. The three men saw them coming toward them. "Good Lord." Stone smiled. "Someone's about to get it. Look at what's coming at us. Any one of them by themselves would be enough for a strong man to handle, but all three at once. God, I hope they're coming for one of you fellows." Chief Sparks immediately started walking away. "Where are you going?"

"I train my officers to know when they're outnumbered. I'm simply following my own advice."

"Coward." Stone shouted after him.

The Chief lifted his elbows. "Cluck. Cluck." He looked back at them. "You boys are on your own. Good luck."

"Stone, will you excuse us? We need to have a word with Henry."

Stone shook his head sadly. "I'm so sorry. Is your last will and testament up to date?" Stone then chuckled and walked away.

The three women encircled Henry. He literally was in a corner. There was no way he could escape. He knew that the conversation was going to go one of two ways. They were going to completely dress him down and let him know he was being an absolute fool, or, they were going to give their approval followed by a ton of unsolicited advice. Henry was both relieved and elated to receive their blessing and the advice.

Shady and the help were in the process of cleaning up. Martha Dexter had managed to gather up some of the leftovers to carry home with her. The girls had retreated to their rooms to play. Delilah and Henry collapsed on the sofa in the living room. "I like your friends, Henry. Everyone was so nice to me."

"You certainly earned their approval. Everyone loved you. Do you remember talking to Stone Clemons and Chief Sparks?"

"I do. They were so gracious. They had me laughing. They're really funny."

A devilish grin spread across Henry's face. "Well, I want you to stay away from those two."

"Why?"

"Those two old fools have the hots for you. There's nothing more dangerous than a couple of old dogs in heat. You have to watch old dogs. They know where to bite."

"Henry, they're crazy about you."

"I know. Just watch yourself around them."

"Well, I noticed that you got cornered for some time by three very lovely older women."

"Some call them the three witches of First Church. I prefer to call them the Three Musketeers."

"Were they giving you advice?"

"They were." Henry turned so that he could look Delilah in the eyes. "They told me that I needed to marry you. They said if I let you get away, then I'm not as smart as they think I am. They thought the sooner the better."

"And what did you tell them?"

"I told them that I would take their counsel under review."

"Is that all?"

"No, I told them that maybe in a year or so there would be a wedding."

Delilah took a deep breath. "Henry, there's something I really need to tell you."

"Oh. What is it?"

Delilah felt herself blushing. "Henry…"

"Go on."

"Henry…you may not want to wait a year to ask me."

"Why not? Are you going somewhere?"

"No, silly. I'm not going anywhere. I don't want to ever leave you."

"Then what is it?"

"It's probably not a very good idea to put the wedding off much longer."

A concerned look washed over Henry's face. "Why, Dee? What are you trying to tell me?"

Dee took in a deep breath. She squeezed Henry's hand and then blurted out the secret she'd been carrying. "Henry, I'm pregnant!"

Henry sat straight up. "That's not possible. I was fixed."

Delilah smiled. "I told the doctor that, but he said sometimes it happens. There's a one in two thousand chance that your vas deferens could reconnect. Guess what, you're one in two thousand."

Henry reached down and lifted Delilah off the couch. "You're sure?"

"I'm sure."

Henry twirled around while he held her. "I'm so happy. We're going to have a baby. I never thought that could happen." He then kissed her passionately.

She pushed herself away from him so that she could look in his eyes. "Henry, do you still want to wait a year to marry me?"

Henry stood looking at her for a minute. Then he knelt down on one knee.

⚘

chapter 36

ALMEDA ALEXANDER DRUMMOND was sitting in the sunroom of her beautiful mansion on River Street reading the morning paper. She had placed the greater portion of the newspaper on the table. Almeda was most interested in reading the society pages first. The Sunday morning paper always recorded the engagement announcements; stories of the weddings celebrated on Saturday and of course there were photos and stories of the various events in society attended by the most important people in the community. Almeda was particularly pleased to see a beautiful picture of her standing with Mary Alice Smythe. They were in charge of planning the upcoming women's bazaar at First Church. It was the largest fundraising event undertaken by the women of the parish. Beyond being a fundraiser it would be preceded by several wonderful social events for the elite of First Church. The black tie banquet to celebrate the bazaar's success was especially enjoyable and received a full page of coverage in the newspaper. The magazine *Life In Falls City* would devote several pages to the banquet.

Almeda had just poured herself another cup of coffee from the silver service her houseboy had placed on the table when her eye fell on another story. It was an obituary. Obituaries are routinely printed on the pages just before the classifieds in the local news section. This particular obituary had earned a spot in the society pages. It was about a woman that had grown up in Falls City but after her marriage moved to Savannah where she had resided until her death. The obituary referenced her education at fine southern schools, her debut, and all of the woman's notable charitable accomplishments. Indeed the woman had lived a life of privilege and position.

Almeda put the paper down. She sat staring out the window at the brightly colored roses surrounding her swimming pool. Not even my beloved Chadsworth's obituary had earned a placement on the society pages. She found this quite troubling. Almeda then resolved that when the time came, her obituary would be placed on the society pages, but how? She had not gone to prestigious schools or even made a debut. She had grown up in Melon Town, Alabama in a smelly house trailer with an abusive father and a drunken mother. It wasn't until after she married Chadsworth that she was able to enter Falls City society. Since her marriage to Horace Drummond, she had managed to retain her position but without the memberships in the country club, exclusive Magnolia Club or the cotillion. Even the Junior League had ceased to invite her to do training. She had retained Chadsworth's last name simply for the doors that it continued to open for her. Still she knew she had lost some of her prestige by marrying Horace. She loved him and all that didn't matter.

Then Almeda began to worry. What if some nosey reporter decided to start digging around in her past after she was gone. It would all just be too humiliating. She would never be able to get over having her life in Melon Town made public. Her past could be revealed after she was dead and there would be nothing she could do to stop it. Absolutely everyone would know that her entire life had been a fraud. A reporter could discover that she had not been a woman of breeding and culture. Even in her grave she just knew she would be mortified if that were to occur. She had to do something to stop it.

Almeda stood and began pacing the floor. She could not leave her obituary to chance. She'd have to write it herself. But beyond that, she wanted to insure that her obituary would be on the society pages. She walked to the writing desk in the sitting room off the master bedroom. She would write her own obituary to insure that it contained the information she wanted it to say about her. No...that wouldn't be enough. She'd personally deliver it to the editor of the newspaper. Even if she had to purchase the space, she was going to have her obituary on the society pages. She took pen and paper from the drawer. She would have her secretary type it after she was satisfied with her writing.

Almeda began. "The entire community has been saddened by the loss of one our leading citizens. Almeda Alexander Drummond passed from this life surrounded by her loving family. Almeda was born into an affluent southern family. Her father was one of the leading physicians in Birmingham, Alabama and held the patents to several life saving medical devices. Her mother came from an old and prestigious Alabama family known for their many charitable contributions throughout the state. Several prominent buildings on medical and educational campuses carry the family name. She was raised in the exclusive society town of Mountain Brook, a beautiful tree lined neighborhood of historic mansions. There she made her debut and was presented to Alabama society before attending and graduating from Mary Baldwin in Virginia. She was a member of Alpha Delta Pi. At Mary Baldwin, Mrs. Alexander Drummond studied interior design and landscaping. She was well known for her design abilities. Women of taste throughout the South often sought after her counsel on these matters. Her beautiful dinner parties were the talk of the social set for weeks after the events. The expansive home on River Street that she owned was a show place and was often featured in magazine articles throughout the nation. The articles elaborated on her excellent taste and the social graces she demonstrated as one of the premier hostesses in the state.

Her first husband, Chadsworth Purcell Alexander, preceded her in death. They were married at the Episcopal Cathedral in Birmingham. Twelve bridesmaids accompanied Almeda at the wedding. It was the social event of that season, attended by one thousand of the leading citizens in the state. Chadsworth and Almeda were both so striking in their appearance and taste that they were often called Falls City's Camelot Couple. They were frequent guests at the Governor's Mansion and the White House in Washington, D. C.

Almeda, with her husband Chadsworth, were members of The Magnolia Club, The Falls City Country Club, The Cotillion, and the Falls City Debutante Society. Almeda was also a trainer for the Junior League. She has served on the board of the Women's Club, The United Fund, and The Falls City Medical Clinic. She was a devout member of

First Church (Episcopal) where she also served on the altar guild, the board of the women of the church, and served as chair of the annual bazaar multiple times.

Her husband, The Reverend Doctor Horace Drummond, an Episcopal priest, survives her. Two sons also survive her from her marriage to Chadsworth Alexander and one adopted son and a stepdaughter with Doctor Drummond.

Almeda was blessed by so many friendships and was loved by all. Almeda enjoyed helping people. She was fondly known for her generosity, kindness, strong spirit and selfless actions.

Hundreds of mourners are expected to attend the service honoring her life and achievements. In lieu of flowers, please send your contributions to the Almeda Alexander Drummond Memorial Fund to be administered by the Altar Guild of First Church. Mrs. Alexander Drummond established that fund prior to her death."

When Almeda had finished writing, she re-read what she had placed on the paper. After her secretary had typed it, she would take it to the editor to retain in his files until her death in thirty years or so. Then a thought struck her. She needed a photograph. She would have to research the very best photographers. Her final photo would simply have to do her justice. Perhaps she should use a photographer in New York City. She wanted someone that was known for their work with fashion models and movie stars. Yes, that is exactly who she needed to take the photo for her obituary. She would settle for no one else. She resolved to contract with a fashion photographer. Almeda sat back in her chair. A feeling of great satisfaction washed over her. Her obituary would appear on the society pages.

<hr />

chapter 37

SEAN EVANS WAS a nervous wreck. The Savannah Auditorium was filling up with people from all over the diocese. Convention delegates, clergy spouses and members of the various boards and committees had been mailed tickets for reserved seats. They were also told that they must be in their seats two hours prior to the service. Separate vesting areas were set-aside for the diocesan clergy, clergy of other denominations, and visiting bishops. The Presiding Bishop and the consecrating bishops would vest in a separate area with Sean. The choir consisted of two hundred and fifty voices from throughout the diocese. The lay participants were to gather in the vesting area with the choir.

"Jim, has there been any sign of that crazy woman?"

Sean had placed Jim Vernon in charge of coordinating all the details for the service. "No sign of her. All the security guards have her picture. They have walkie-talkies. I am in communication with them on this one. If she shows, I'll let you know."

"But what if she doesn't show up until after the service begins?"

"Sean, you've got to accept the fact that we're going to do everything we can to make sure she doesn't get in here. There's always the chance that she will. The Presiding Bishop has all the facts. If by chance the woman gets by us and stands to make an objection at the time appointed in the service, we have a plan. I will be next to the Presiding Bishop. I will make sure the woman doesn't have access to a microphone, so no one in the convention center will be able to hear a word she says. When's she's finished, the Presiding Bishop will simply dismiss her saying that her allegations have already been investigated and were found to be false. If the woman refuses to be seated, we'll have the security guards escort her out of the building. I have everything under control. Please calm down and enjoy your ordination."

Sean felt himself relax. "Okay, walk me through the service one more time."

Jim handed Sean a chart. "The choir is not going to process. It will already be in place. I recruited the local newscaster to read the opening sentence that will start the service. Honest to God, Sean, this guy's voice sounds just like Charlton Heston. The congregation is going to think that God Himself is speaking. He is going to read these words from the Book of Acts: *They were all together in one place. And suddenly from heaven there came a sound like the rush of a violent wind, and it filled the entire house where they were sitting.* At that point the two synthesizers will start playing the sound of wind blowing through the sound system."

Sean smiled. "That sounds great."

"It's going to be so moving. The first three thurifers will enter. They will walk down the center aisle. One thurifer will lead the other two. Then will come a crucifer surrounded by four torches. Then follows the various lay participants."

"The sound of the wind is still blowing?"

"At about this point the organ will begin to improvise on the opening hymn while the sound of the wind continues."

"I'm getting goose pimples just thinking about it."

"Next comes the clergy cross surrounded by four torches. It will be preceded by a thurifer. The clergy from each parish in the diocese will process, preceded by a banner bearer carrying their parish banner. At this point the timpani will begin to roll and the orchestra will join the wind and the organ in the prepared fanfare and prelude."

"Wow, that really sounds dramatic."

"Oh, Sean, hold on. You haven't heard it all. The youth of the diocese have prepared these giant streamers on the end of these long flexible poles. They're going to come down every aisle of the auditorium waving the streamers in the air over the people. At that point another thurifer will enter followed by the visiting clergy cross, torches, and all the visiting clergy."

"I've got to see that."

"Sorry, you'll be at the end of the procession but you can see it when you enter the auditorium. The teenagers are going to stand in place waving the streamers over the congregation until after the opening hymn has ended."

"What's next?"

"Another thurifer, cross and torches will enter followed by all the visiting bishops."

"Did you tell them I wanted them to wear their copes and mitres?"

"All of them will except the one from up there in Virginia. He doesn't even own one."

"His problem. I think it will be really colorful in spite of him."

"Then the last thurifer, a cross and four torches leading the diocesan banner. Bishop Petersen will follow the banner followed by your co-consecrators; then I will lead you in. The Presiding Bishop will come last, led by a chaplain."

"God, Jim you've done a great job." Sean embraced him.

"Later, big boy."

"Is that any way to talk to your bishop?"

"Oh, you just wait."

"Back to the service."

"The hymn will not begin until everyone is in place. You and I both agree that it doesn't make sense to put together a beautiful procession and then ask people to bury their faces in a hymnal. You know how the rest of the service goes."

It was a beautiful service for the ordination of a bishop. Everything was done with decency and in order. There was no sign of the woman that wanted to keep Sean from becoming a bishop. When the Presiding Bishop asked if there were any objections, the question was met with silence. As his first act as the Bishop of Savannah, Sean blessed the twenty-five hundred people that filled the auditorium. Sean quickly changed out of his new cope and mitre so that he could escort the Presiding Bishop to the reception across the street in the Hyatt Ballroom. On their way out the front door, the new Bishop Evans spotted two sets of demonstrators being kept on opposite sides of the street by police and police barricades. On the one side was a group carrying rainbow flags and placards proclaiming messages of love. There were signs demanding the legalization of gay marriage. On the other side of the street was a group of protesters carrying signs with scriptural verses on them condemning homosexual acts. Other signs declared homosexuality to be a sin. There were even a couple calling on The Episcopal Church to repent. The two groups were shouting at each other. Neither even took notice of the two bishops walking between them. Then Sean spotted Jim.

"How did you do this?"

"I made a couple of telephone calls. I let the pastors of a couple of Bible Churches know that the Episcopal Church would be having a big service at the auditorium. I suggested that it would be a good time for his congregation to witness to the great sin of homosexuality."

Sean smiled. "You sly dog."

"The best way to neutralize one side is to balance it with the polar opposite."

Sean slapped Jim on the back. "You're amazing."

chapter 38

TRAVIS WAS CONSTANTLY pulling on his daddy's hand. He wanted to move to the next attraction. From the time they bought their tickets and walked through the gates at Disneyland in Anaheim, California, Travis was a bundle of excitement. Randi was successful in getting him to stand still long enough to have his picture made in front of the large flower mural of Mickey Mouse at the entrance. Their best friends Rob and Melanie went with them to the park. Rob was the official photographer. Even though both Rob and Melanie lived in California they'd never been to Disneyland. Now with their godchild, Amanda, visiting they seized on the opportunity to go. While Amanda would see most of the park from her stroller when she wasn't napping, Rob and Melanie were excited to see the attraction through Travis' eyes.

Main Street Disney welcomed them with a trolley car. Travis pulled them all aboard for the circular ride down one side of Main Street and back up the other. When they disembarked, a larger than life size Pluto character was standing surrounded by admiring fans. Smiling parents quickly snapped pictures of their gleeful offspring with the infamous dog. To Steele and Randi's surprise, Travis was unimpressed. He remembered the Dumbo ride. It was one they'd had a difficult time removing him from the last time they were at Disneyland. Travis pulled them past the carousel to Dumbo. This time he was content with a single ride. It was back to the carousel. Steele held Amanda on one of the horses while Travis and the rest of the party each claimed a horse of their own.

Lunch was eaten at the pizza pavilion in Tomorrow Land. Then they were off to Frontier Land for a ride on the riverboat. Randi vetoed Steele's suggestion of the haunted house in New Orleans Square. She also vetoed Pirates of the Caribbean. So it was back to Fantasy Land for Mister Toad's Wild Ride. They found great seats for the parade. Amanda slept. Steele held Travis in his arms for the entire parade. Travis pointed and clapped as the various Disney characters passed in review. Following the parade, Randi and Melanie put in a demand for some real food. They found a cafeteria at the end of Main Street. Then to Travis' absolute delight, he spotted Winnie the Pooh and Tigger posing for hugs and photographs. Steele and Rob made sure that Travis had ample opportunity for both.

The women wanted to browse through some of the shops lining Main Street. Financially, this proved to be a disaster. Travis latched onto a stuffed replica of Winnie the Pooh that was actually bigger than he was. Steele quickly checked the price tag and tried to divert Travis' attention elsewhere. After some prolonged and tearful screaming, Steele relented and bought Travis the Winnie the Pooh.

Back at Rob and Melanie's house, Travis was fast asleep in one of the guest rooms with his arm wrapped around Winnie. Amanda was sleeping in another bedroom that had been set up as a nursery complete with a baby bed.

Melanie and Randi were sitting at the kitchen table. Melanie had opened a bottle of white wine for them. Rob and Steele were sitting out on the patio by the pool enjoying their evening cocktails. Rob's English Bulldog, Winston, was keeping them company.

"That's got to be the cutest ugly dog I've ever seen." Randi smiled.

"Oh, you know Rob. He's a big guy and he likes big toys. He's absolutely devoted to that dog. I did draw the line at letting him sleep on our bed."

"I'd have a hard time with that as well. " Randi agreed. "There's just something about him. The only words I can come up with to describe him are *ugly cute*." Randi enjoyed another sip of wine. "Melanie, this wine is wonderful. Where did you get it?"

"It's from one of our favorite little wineries up in the Central Coastal Valley. Rob has become quite the connoisseur."

"Does he consider himself to be an oenophile?"

Melanie chuckled. "No, he's not that precise. Oenophiles know all about the soil the grapes are grown in. They're experts on the amount of rainfall and the year the grapes were harvested and all that stuff."

"It's so good. It must have really been expensive."

"Not really. Only those in wine cults buy the really expensive bottles."

"Wine cults?"

Melanie topped off each of their glasses. "Those are the folks that will only drink wine that costs several hundred dollars a bottle or more. They're usually on expense accounts. Most of the time they just want to impress people with the price tag. There are certain vineyards that are more than happy to help them spend their money."

"Is it really that much better?"

"Not if you ask me, but then I don't like caviar either. I guess we've become wine enthusiasts. We only buy the wines we really like that we consider to be reasonably priced."

"The only thing I know about wine is that I really like this one."

Melanie hesitated and then asked, "So what do you think he's going to do?"

"When we left Pawleys Island we'd both pretty much agreed that we wanted to move back to Oklahoma. Steele is thinking about selling real estate. We could be close to our families. We have lots of friends there. I think he's just had enough. He doesn't want to do this anymore."

"It's a real shame. He's so good at it. He's one of the best preachers I've ever heard. Just look at all the good he's done for the poor in Falls City. I'm certain they'll never give him credit for bringing that dead church to life."

"I know you're right, but is it worth it? That church almost destroyed our marriage."

"You could have done a lot to prevent that."

"I know. I should have listened to you."

"How do you feel about it all?"

"I'm tired of living in a glass house. I'm tired of everyone having an opinion about how we should live and what we should do. It's as though they think we are a national park or something. I'd like to walk around with a big sign that says, *We're not a part of the public domain.*"

"So you won't mind if he's not running a parish?"

"I just know I'm tired. I know Steele is beginning to feel better, but he's still not himself."

"Would you consider living here in California?"

"We hadn't even considered that possibility."

"You know Rob works for my father's company. He's really doing quite well. He loves what he's doing. I could talk to daddy to see if he could find a place for Steele."

"Gosh, I don't know what Steele would think about that. "

"Do you want me to ask Steele if he'd consider it? Would you like that?"

Randi considered the idea for a minute. She'd looked forward to moving closer to her parents, but then Rob and Melanie were their best friends. "Let's have Rob approach Steele with the idea. I'm afraid if it comes from you he'll reject it, mistaking it for pity."

"That's probably a better idea. Rob and I have talked about it. I'll have him approach Steele."

"Does Rob work tomorrow?"

"No, he's off… off like a Prom dress." Melanie giggled.

"I was thinking that maybe he could go ahead and ask Steele. If he agrees, Rob could ask your father tomorrow at work."

"Well, he can just call daddy in the morning if Steele agrees to the idea."

"That sounds good. Speaking of ideas. It was awfully nice of you to get a baby crib for Amanda to sleep in. You didn't need to fix up a nursery for her."

"About that…there's something I've been wanting to ask you. I guess there's no time like the present."

"Okay."

"Remember, I told you that Rob and I have been trying to have a baby."

"You told me you were trying." Tears began streaming down Melanie's cheeks. "Melanie, what's wrong?" Randi reached across the table and took her hand.

Melanie wiped her eyes with a tissue. "We can't have a baby."

"Oh no, I'm so sorry."

"We found out that Rob is sterile."

"But that's not possible, Melanie. He has a son."

Melanie nodded. "You know that his wife was murdered by a lover."

"Yes, I remember."

"Well, evidently it wasn't the first time she'd cheated on Rob."

"You don't mean...?"

"It's been a lot for Rob to digest. He'd always had the feeling that he wasn't the boy's father but he chose not to deal with it."

"How? I mean...I don't know what I mean."

"You've met his son. He's thin and frail like his mother. Rob is big, muscular and athletic. His son doesn't have an athletic bone in his body. He is more interested in books than sports. He doesn't even look like Rob."

"Has that changed his relationship with him?"

"Not one bit. Rob said, 'I raised him and I've loved him from the first time I held him. It's love that makes families, not blood.' "

"So have you thought about adopting?"

Melanie grimaced. "We have, but I'd really like to experience pregnancy. Rob understands that. So we're thinking about an insemination."

"Have you started?"

"We looked into it, but it just seemed so impersonal choosing a donor father from a computer file."

"I can only imagine. So what do you think you're going to do?"

Melanie stared into Randi's eyes. "Randi, we're best friends. I love you like a sister. I wouldn't be comfortable asking anyone else in the world this question but you."

"What?"

"Please don't get upset with me. And please don't let this affect our friendship. We're still going to be friends no matter what."

"Melanie, what do you want to ask me?"

"Randi, Rob and I have talked about this a lot. It's not a crazy idea and we're not asking it in desperation."

"For God's sake, Melanie. What is it you want to ask me?"

Melanie was nervously twisting the tissue that she'd wiped her eyes with. "Randi, would you agree to let Steele be the donor for our baby?"

Randi felt everything go dark. She actually believed she may have passed out while she was still sitting up. "Melanie...gosh...Melanie, I don't know. I mean...why Steele?"

"Well you have to admit that man knows how to make pretty babies." The two women giggled, releasing some of the tension in the room. "We love both you guys. We know you. We would much rather share this experience with you than with some anonymous stranger."

Randi's mind was blank. She really didn't know what to say. "I'm going to have to discuss this with Steele." Randi turned toward the patio. She could see Rob and Steele laughing. "Is Rob going to bring this up with Steele?"

"No, we both agreed that I would start with you. If you have any problem with it, then there would be no need to even approach Steele with the idea."

"Melanie, I don't think I can give you an answer either direction. I just have to talk to Steele. Right this minute I can't tell you how I feel about it. You're just going to have to give me some time."

"I understand. Take all the time you need." Melanie walked over to the wine cabinet and brought another bottle to the table. "I think maybe we both could use this. I know you're going to like it. This wine was a gift from one of Rob's business associates. He's an enthusiastic member of the wine cult."

So it's expensive?"

"Very."

"Do you think it's worth it?"

"Well, let's drink it and then you tell me."

⚭

chapter 39

NED BOONE, JUDITH, and Elmer Idle were standing under the large live oak trees that formed a natural umbrella over the patio at Saint Andrew's Presbyterian Church. As they drank their coffee they critiqued the morning worship service.

"It appears to me that there were more people in church this morning than any Sunday we've been here." Ned observed.

"I think you're right, Ned." Elmer chimed in. "I think the senior pastor was holding the church back."

"Well, how many do you know that stay away from First Church because of Steele Austin?"

"Point well made. It only makes sense that there are a lot that have stayed away from this place because of that preacher. Now that he's gone they're coming back."

"Well, I just wish that we could sing more uplifting hymns." Judith whined. "All these Presbyterian hymns just sound like a funeral dirge. Don't they believe in being joyful? Our God is a wondrous God. We need to praise Him with uplifting music." Judith then lifted her hands. "We've not sung one song that made me want to lift my hands in praise."

"Have you made a pledge yet, Ned?" Elmer asked.

"No, and I don't plan on doing so until I see who they hire as the new preacher. If I like him I'll make a pledge. If I don't, I'll just give a couple of dollars when I attend."

"Judith and I haven't made a pledge either. I put a twenty in the plate this morning."

Ned gave Elmer a disapproving look. "I saw you do that. I don't think that's necessary. Until they get a new preacher and he meets our approval, I just plan on continuing to throw a couple of bucks in the plate when I attend. That's a gracious plenty. I haven't even seen a budget. I have no idea how they're spending the money. Have you seen a copy of the budget?"

"No I haven't, Ned. That's a good point. For all we know they could be taking our hard earned money and giving it to the National Council of Churches or some other communist organization."

"Or worse. They could be giving it to help a bunch of queers."

Elmer shuffled his feet and looked at his wife. "Judith, honey. Ned makes a good point. Until we get more information and approve of the new preacher, I think maybe we'll just follow Ned's lead and put a couple of bucks in the plate each week."

"Well, you're the spiritual head of our family. As my husband, your decision is final, but we've always tithed. The Bible instructs us to tithe."

"You're right about that. Tell you what we'll do. We'll put our tithe in a separate fund in our bank. We'll hold it there until we have all the facts about this place. If we approve of everything, then we'll pay our tithe to the church all at one time. If not, we'll give our tithe other places."

"That's a wonderful idea. I can name several wonderful organizations that are Christ-centered that we could support."

Ned grunted. "You'd better make sure that they are Christ-centered. So many of them fly under that banner while giving their money to drunks, drug addicts, and folks too lazy to work."

"We'll take your advice, Ned, and make sure our money goes where we want it to go."

"Well, how'd you folks enjoy the service this morning?" Harlan McMurray approached them with an outstretched hand.

"I sure hope you don't have plans to hire that associate pastor as your main guy." Ned barked.

"Goodness no. He's a good second fiddle but he could never play first chair."

"Well, I'm relieved to hear that."

"Can't we sing more uplifting music?" Judith asked, wide eyed.

"Our choirmaster keeps a pretty tight rein on the music program. Every time the membership has asked that question he's threatened to quit. It's his way or the highway."

"Well then, let him quit. Better yet, fire him and hire one that will play what the congregation wants to sing." Ned's eyes grew wide with anger. "I'm sick and tired of these preachers and musicians thinking they're in charge of the church. They're here to do what we want them to do. We're the bosses and they're the employees. If we want to sing Yankee Doodle on Sunday morning, then it's their job to play it."

"I just wish that the pastoral prayer didn't have to be so long. Goodness, that preacher prayed for everyone but Roy Rogers and his horse Trigger this morning."

Harlan couldn't contain his laughter. "That man sure likes the sound of his own voice, doesn't he? I'll have a word with the president of the session. I agree. He doesn't need to tell the Lord everything he knows."

"My hunch is that he wasn't even talking to the Lord." Ned mumbled.

"Now I hate to disagree with you gentlemen, because I understand that a husband is the head of the wife and women should keep quiet in the church." Judith rebutted. "But the Bible instructs us to pray without ceasing. I thought the pastoral prayer was wonderful."

Ned cleared his throat. "The Sunday service is only supposed to last one hour. Today's service was one hour and fourteen minutes. If they'd left out the pastoral prayer completely, the service would have ended on time."

"How's the search for a new preacher going?" Elmer asked.

"I'm so glad that you asked that question. The session has asked me to chair the search committee to find our next senior minister."

Ned brightened. "You get to choose the next preacher?"

"Well, my committee will choose the next preacher. I will be their leader."

"Who's on your committee?"

"I'm still in the process of putting the committee together. I want it to be a real cross-section of our parish."

"I think that's a wonderful idea." Judith smiled. "Elmer and I will add you and the committee to our daily prayer time."

"Thank you, Judith." Harlan acknowledged. "I was hoping that I could get one of you to serve on the committee with me. As our newest members, you would bring a unique perspective."

"How much power does the committee have?" Ned asked.

"I guess we have all the power we need. We will receive nominations from the congregation and we're also free to seek out clergy we want to interview."

"That sounds good." Ned nodded.

"Well, can I get one of you to serve on the committee?"

Judith spoke first. "I think it should be you, Ned. You have a sixth sense about preachers. You're really able to discern which ones are true men of God and which are phonies. You were one of the first to discern that Steele Austin was no man of God. It's a spiritual gift. I think you should do it."

"I agree with Judith." Elmer was elated. "Harlan, I nominate Ned Boone."

"Ned, will you be on the search committee to find the next senior pastor for Saint Andrews Presbyterian Church?"

Ned agreed. As he drove home from Saint Andrew's Presbyterian Church that morning, he could not stop smiling.

⊙⩗⊙

chapter 40

BISHOP SEAN EVANS and his Canon, Jim Vernon, had just finished saying their morning prayers together and were sitting down to breakfast. "I just love it when I sleep over and we get to have breakfast together."

Sean nodded, "I do too, Jim."

Jim leaned across the table and kissed Sean on the lips. "What's on your schedule today?"

"I've got a full day of appointments. I'm beginning to see what Bishop Petersen meant when he said that he often felt like the office was holding him a prisoner."

"Are any of them appointments you could send to me?"

"I don't see how. They call for an appointment with the Bishop. If I send them down the hall to my Canon, I just don't think that will go over."

"I noticed a couple of suits from Falls City in your office yesterday."

"Yeah, it was a Stone Clemons and the chief of the police department."

"Clemons. He walks softly down there but he swings a big club. Why did he bring the chief of police with him? They've already had one scandal with a crooked administrator. I pray to God they're not having another."

"Would you and Reverend Vernon like anything else, Bishop?" Clarence had been in the laundry room. He had started the laundry after fixing their breakfast.

"No, Clarence. This is very good though. Thanks so much."

"Yes suh, bishop. I'ma gonna run the sweeper now in the living room."

"Thanks, Clarence."

"How'd you get Clarence to come work for you?" Jim asked after taking a sip of coffee.

"Bishop Petersen called me and asked me if I was going to employ any house *Help*. He sang Clarence's praise. I don't know why he felt the need to tell me but he told me Clarence could be trusted to keep his own counsel. He would never repeat to anyone anything he saw or heard."

"He seems like a really nice fellow."

"I'm pleased with him. He'd worked for Bishop Petersen for years. He just felt really bad about leaving him unemployed."

"Well, I'm glad you have him. Now back to your visitors from Falls City. What's up with them?"

"You remember the rector is on sabbatical. You'll also remember that Bishop Petersen removed the senior warden."

Jim smiled and shook his head. "You just got to admire the little man for that. Frankly, I didn't think he had it in him."

"Well, the vestry at the last meeting amended the by-laws to make it possible for the rector to appoint the senior warden. They don't have one right now and they are without a rector to appoint one."

"So what did you tell them?"

"I told them that in the absence of a rector the Canons make it clear that the bishop of the diocese becomes the rector."

"I have a hunch Clemons already knew that. I think he's a self-taught canon lawyer in his own right."

Sean smiled. "And so he is. I discovered that within minutes of their arrival."

"So what did you do?"

"I made two appointments."

"Two?"

"I appointed the chief of police, Sparks is his name, as senior warden."

"You didn't?"

"Oh, but I did. I asked Stone Clemons to be my new diocesan chancellor. He agreed."

"That, my friend, is a stroke of political genius. Steele Austin will be delighted."

"What do you have going today?"

Jim pushed his plate away and opened the portfolio he'd placed on the floor beneath his chair. He brought out a file. The mission down in Dale has lost their vicar. He was called to be rector of a parish up in North Carolina. We need to appoint a new vicar. I have some possible names for you to look at right here."

"Just like that? You mean I choose the vicar without even discussing it with the congregation?"

"That's your privilege as the bishop. That's exactly how it was done under Petersen."

Sean pushed his chair back from the table and crossed his arms and legs. "Jim, I want to make some changes and I think this would be a good place to begin."

"What sort of changes?"

"I've learned that the clergy in this diocese didn't trust Bishop Petersen. In fact, many of them felt like he abused them. I want to change that. I want them to see me as their pastor and not as some sort of dictator. I want to earn their trust and that of the laity."

"What did you have in mind?"

"This is a good place to begin. I guess you've screened the candidates you had in mind for this position."

"Well, none of them are going to set the world on fire, but they're all solid priests. They can handle that mission."

"Okay, I want you to meet with the mission committee. I want you to give them the names and the contact information. Tell them to interview the candidates and decide which one they'd like for me to appoint. Once they've decided, I'll meet with them and the candidate together to discuss their mutual ministry."

"Wow, Sean, that's going to be quite a change."

"It's only the beginning. I'm learning this diocese has a reputation in the larger Church and it's not a favorable one. I want to change that as well. I am calling a meeting of all the priests and the senior wardens.

I want to make it clear that the days of abusing clergy in this diocese are over."

"What about the clergy that really do need to move on?"

"Then we'll work to gain their cooperation with that and we'll work with them to find positions more suitable, but we will not be sending them out into that dark night without a place to go."

"Bishop, the telephone is for you."

"Thanks, Clarence." He took the portable phone from him.

"I enjoyed your consecration, Bishop Evans." Sean snapped his fingers for Jim to pick up the kitchen extension. "I'm so glad that you did."

"Now, what are your plans for our community?"

"I beg your pardon. What do you mean our community?"

"Yours and mine, Bishop. Our gay brothers and sisters want to know what you're going to do to open the doors of opportunity in the Church for us."

"What doors in particular did you have in mind?"

"Oh, come. Let's not play games."

"Look, I don't know who you are but I am new to this job. I can assure you that I am going to do everything in my power to see that people in this diocese are not discriminated against for any reason."

"Well, let's just see that you do. I'll be watching. Just like that birthmark on your right butt cheek…I'm closer than you think." Then the line went dead.

Sean looked at Jim. "What are we going to do about him?"

"Frankly, I don't think we have to do anything. Your caller ID doesn't show his number. It just reads blocked call. As soon as I get to the office I'm going to have the telephone company add blocked call service to your phones. Anyone that calls will have to reveal their name and number or the call won't go through."

"Thanks, Jim. That's a really good idea." Sean stared at the table as though he was trying to read some invisible message on it.

"What's on your mind?"

"Oh, I don't know. I was just thinking that first I had some looney woman giving me grief. Now I have some prancing queen after me. Where is this going to end?"

Jim winked at Sean. "*My Lord Bishop.* I think this is only the beginning."

chapter 41

"IT'S JUST TOO weird, Randi. I just think that's all we need to tell them."
Randi and Steele had taken Travis to the beach. Melanie volunteered to
keep Amanda at the house.

"What's weird is how dark you've gotten. Between the sun at
Pawleys and now the sun here in California you look like a native. I
think I'd better put a glow-in-the-dark headband on you before letting
you out at night."

"This is the color I was most all the time before I got an indoor
job. I could get used to this California weather."

"What did Rob tell you about the job?"

"Well, there is no job right now. He and Melanie are just willing
to talk to her father to see if he could find me a position."

"I think it would be a lot more expensive living out here than in
Oklahoma."

"If I could only make half of what Rob told me he made last year
we'd more than double what I made at First Church. We wouldn't be
able to afford a house in Beverly Hills like they have, but we'd be doing
better than we ever have."

"Sounds good to me."

"So you're in favor of doing this?"

"I don't think it hurts to talk. It would really be great to be near
Rob and Melanie. I think a lot of it depends on the job. Putting the
money aside, if it means you'd have to do something you wouldn't enjoy
doing, then I think we should reconsider."

"I agree. I'll tell Rob that we'd at least like to know what's available and then we'll take it from there."

They watched Travis running back and forth from the water's edge to a little hole in the sand that he and Steele had dug with his plastic shovel. He was filling his sand bucket with ocean water and running to dump the water in the hole. "I don't think we're going to have any trouble getting him to go to sleep tonight." Steele smiled and snapped a photo of him with his camera. He then turned to snap a photo of Randi. She threw her arm up, shot him a big smile, and posed.

"You are so beautiful." He leaned over and kissed her.

"Even after two children you still think I'm beautiful?"

"I'm going to think that you're the most beautiful woman in the world when we're one of those wrinkled old couples sitting in church holding hands."

"Speaking of wrinkles. Have you noticed these around my mouth?"

Steele stared at her. "Randi, growing older is inevitable. I spotted some gray hair in the mirror a few days ago. It's going to happen. Just remember that when I married you I didn't ask you to come and stay young with me. I asked you to come and grow old with me."

"A tear dropped from Randi's eye. "Oh, Steele. To think those jackasses almost destroyed our marriage. I don't see how you could even think about going back."

"Right now I'm not. We still have four months left. Let's consider all our options. But as of this minute it's California by six touchdowns. Falls City has zip."

"But you haven't completely given up on going back, have you?"

"Not yet, but I'm close. There is something I'd like to do."

"What?"

"I'd like to go up to San Francisco."

"That could be fun. Maybe Rob and Melanie would like to go along and we could make a weekend of it."

"Randi, it's something I'd like to do alone. Once I have this out of the way, then maybe we could all go back another time."

"What is it, Steele? You're making me nervous."

"No secrets, Randi. I'd like to follow up on a hunch that's been gnawing at me for some time now."

"Steele, you're still not thinking you'll be able to find Chadsworth, are you? We've already been through that a dozen times. Let it go."

"Listen to me, Randi. Do you remember that Horace told us that the chair of the standing committee in that diocese called him? He offered to help Horace after it was discovered that Elmer Idle had rigged the election against him."

"I remember."

"Randi, he said his name was Earl Lafitte. Earl Lafitte was the name of Chadsworth's lover in Atlanta. I think that Chadsworth has assumed his identity. If I can find Earl Lafitte, I will find Chadsworth."

"And then what?"

"I think he wants me to find him. He's just left too many breadcrumbs along my ministry trail. There have been too many coincidences."

Randi drew in a deep breath. "Okay, Steele. Do what you need to do, but could this please be that last time you go on a ghost chase?"

"If I don't find him this time. I'll let it go."

"Now, I think we should talk some more about Melanie and Rob's request.

"Oh, honey, it's just too weird. I mean, what if we want to have another baby?"

Melanie broke out laughing. "Steele, it's not like you're going to run out of supply."

He chuckled. "I know. You really think that we should do this?"

"What do you mean we?"

"What's mine is yours, Randi."

"Yes, and don't you forget it."

"Okay. Let's talk about it. How would you feel being around a child that you knew I had fathered with another woman?"

"She's not another woman. She's my best friend. I love her like a sister. And you and Rob are two peas in a pod."

"I love both of them, but Randi, I just don't know. I think it could be harder on you than me."

"Steele, if you'd had a baby with a wife before me, don't you think I would love that child just like it was my own?"

"Yes, because I know you. You've got one of the most loving and giving hearts I've ever known."

"Okay, shoe on the other foot. How would it feel to see a child that you know you sired call Rob *daddy?*"

"Would they ever tell him who his biological father is?"

"First, what makes you think it would be a him? You have produced one very beautiful daughter. And second, I think that's a question that we need to ask Rob and Melanie. In fact, it may be the best question we can ask them before we make a decision."

"Let's say you were that child. You become an adult and your parents tell you that you were an insemination. Would you want to know?"

"Steele, they do television specials on these children. They are desperate to meet their biological parents. Adopted children have the same need. Wouldn't it be better to discover that your biological donor father was your godfather? Wouldn't it be better to know that he's someone you've known your entire life? That he's loved you and been a part of your world from the moment you were born? That's the bottom line for Rob and Melanie. They think that would be so much better than having their child have to chase down some anonymous donor through some computer bank. The donor center may or may not even be in business when their baby reaches adulthood."

"I guess I hadn't thought about it like that." Steele stared off toward the horizon. "It sounds to me like you want me to do it."

"I think I'm leaning that direction more than you are."

"I just need you to be one hundred percent sure and I need to be there as well. Are you that certain?"

"No. Not yet."

"Good, because neither am I. Have you prayed about it?"

"Little else since Melanie asked me."

"As you know, I haven't been able to pray since we left Falls City. Just maybe this decision will reconnect me with God. I'll pray about it as well. But for right now, let's decide not to decide."

"Agreed. Just know that Melanie told me they want us to stay with them as long as we want, regardless of what we decide."

"That's good, since we really don't have any other place to go."

"We're still going to Oklahoma to see our parents, aren't we?"

"Of course, but Randi, we have to agree right now that if we decide to do this thing with Rob and Melanie, we will not tell your parents or mine. My God, your marine corps sergeant father will castrate me."

"Good one, Steele. You know what? I just think he would."

"You got that straight."

"When are you going to go to San Francisco?"

"Soon."

chapter 42

ALMEDA ALEXANDER DRUMMOND had not been able to convince her husband, Horace, to make many of the changes she wanted at First Church. He was the rector. Or at least he was the rector while Steele Austin was away. She had tried every method she'd known. Her womanly wiles in the bedroom had failed her. Her expertise in the kitchen had not worked either. She was left to the only resource at her disposal. She had tried reasoning with him. To her utter amazement, she discovered that when confronted with logic and facts, he came over to her way of thinking. Who would have known? She mentally kicked herself for all the years of game playing she'd undertaken in an effort to get her way with not one but two husbands.

She was mentally celebrating her most recent victory while getting dressed in her dressing closet. The sun had not yet risen. It was still dark outside. Horace was sleeping and she did not want to wake him. He'd received a call near two in the morning to go to the bedside of a dying parishioner. He did not return home until just before five. She knew he had a meeting at nine. She'd set the alarm for him for seven-thirty. She wanted him to sleep.

As Almeda pulled into the circular driveway in front of First Church she spotted the lawn maintenance crew's truck. Even though this victory forced her from her own peaceful slumber at daybreak once a week, it was well worth it. She had convinced Horace that the two church sextons just didn't have the time and energy to care for both the inside and the exterior grounds of the parish property. She'd brought him several bids from lawn care companies. Finally, he agreed that if the sextons could devote all their energies to the inside, a lawn crew of a half dozen men could make quick work of the church grounds and cemetery. Almeda knew that in spite of their ability, they still needed her supervision. So once a week she would arrive when they did to oversee their work.

They were at the far end of the cemetery. She started walking that direction. She spotted two brightly colored bouquets of flowers on one of the graves. Even from a distance she knew that they were not real. She also knew the graves that hosted them. She stormed toward the graves. She was right. It was Willie and Grace's grave. She put her hands on her hips. She could almost feel the smoke coming out of her ears. The number of times that she'd sent letters to their grandsons telling them that they could not put plastic flowers on the graves in First Church cemetery. She was just disgusted. As she stood staring at the graves she found herself reading the marker. In comparison to the typical marker in the cemetery this one was so simple and quite small. Her eyes fell on the inscription, "Home at last." In spite of her anger she felt her eyes flood with tears. Steele Austin had fought so hard to have a person of color buried in this cemetery. She realized that he'd done it for Willie and Grace but he'd also done it for her Horace. He'd done it for all us.

"Do you want me to throw these flowers away?" It was one of the lawn crew.

Almeda wiped her eyes and shook her head. "No. They're fine. Just leave them. You might take them out and shake the dust off, but then put them back."

"Yes, ma'am. You're the boss."

"I want you to make sure that your men blow off all these head-stones with their blowers. Last week, in spite of my explicit instructions, I saw grass clippings lying on some of these stones. I'll not tolerate that."

"I'll see to it. Anything else?"

"Yes, before you leave today, I want you to meet me up by the big magnolia in front of the church. I want to trim off some of those branches. I also want to make sure your men clean underneath it."

"That'll be the last thing we do. It'll be a couple of hours before we get up there."

"Just make sure you don't leave before talking to me. I'm going to walk the grounds. There just might be some additional work that needs to be done."

"I'll meet you at the magnolia in a couple of hours."

Almeda continued to slowly survey the grounds. There were so many familiar names on the gravestones. Through the years she'd attended many of the funerals of the people buried here. They had become like family to her. First Church was the family she never had growing up. Chadsworth had made all this possible for her. He'd brought her from Melon Town, Alabama to this beautiful South Georgia city. Here he had introduced her to society. He'd actually refined her social skills and provided her with a wonderful life. She owed him so much. Almeda turned her attention toward his grave. When she arrived, she bent down and with her hand dusted the leaves away that had fallen on his marker. She remained on her knees, reading the familiar words over and over again.

Chadsworth Purcell Alexander III
"In his Sixtieth year on earth
He was finally set free."

"Oh, Chadsworth." She grieved. "Whatever did you mean? I still don't understand. Why did you do it? Why did you leave me?" Almeda sat back on the ground. She put her legs to her side and with one hand stroked the grass beneath his marker. "I know that you really liked Mister Austin." She whispered. "You'd be so happy to know that I've grown quite fond of him as well. He's like a son to me. He's done a wonderful job here under some very difficult circumstances. Not only has he built up our church, but he's done so much for the poor in our town. I know just how much you'd approve of all that. I hope you won't mind, Chadsworth, but I've taken some of the money you left me and put it in an irrevocable trust fund for his children. It's for their education. I just felt like it was the least I could do after all he'd done for you and all that he's done for me. Horace approved. He thought it was a good thing. I have a feeling that you'd be agreeable as well." Time continued to slip away as Almeda continued to chat with Chadsworth. It was something she hadn't done since he died. She knew the visit was long overdue.

Her legs had gone to sleep when she finally struggled to her feet. She felt a little lightheaded as she started walking toward the magnolia tree. She opened the watch locket she was wearing on a gold chain around her neck. She realized that the lawn crew would be meeting her at the magnolia tree any minute now. She forced herself to walk faster but thought her legs felt awfully heavy. She was also a bit breathless. She decided that she was just a bit too old to be squatting on the ground. The squatting wasn't the problem, she told herself, it was the getting up. By the time she reached the magnolia tree she was pretty winded. She decided to sit down on the park bench that she'd placed near the tree years ago. She thought perhaps it was time to have it painted again. Suddenly Almeda felt nauseated. She tried to remember what she'd eaten. She broke out in a cold sweat and felt herself being overwhelmed with dizziness. She thought it best to simply lie down on the bench until it all passed. She lay on her back and put her arm up over her forehead. Her heart was pounding. She felt herself struggling for air. She tried to sit up so that she could wave to one of the yardmen to come to her aid, but she was just too weak. She lay back on the bench. Everything around her was beginning to spin out of control. Panic rose up in her chest. She needed air. She desperately needed some air. She could hear herself gasping. Almeda thought if she would just lay still that would be the best thing for her. She closed her eyes but the dizziness did not abate. Then she saw Chadsworth standing above her. He stretched out his hand for her to take. She saw herself stand and take his hand. She was so happy. Together they began to walk hand in hand toward the magnolia tree. There was so much she wanted to share with him. "Chadsworth...Chadsworth..." She was struggling to say his name.

Almeda opened her eyes. He was gone. She looked up at the sky. Her gaze dropped to the magnolia tree sitting so majestically in front of her beloved church. The sun was just breaking over the top of the tree. "How beautiful," she muttered. She'd never before seen the magnolia at sunrise. Then the world of Almeda Alexander Drummond faded into darkness.

Epilogue

STEELE TOOK A taxi from the airport to Grace Cathedral. He'd decided to wear a clerical collar and dark suit. He thought that might serve his purposes best. He walked around the cathedral until he saw a sign pointing to the Dean's Office. He opened the door and was immediately greeted by a receptionist. "May I help you, Father?"

"I'm hoping that you can. I feel so stupid. I've come all the way from the east coast. I am a very old friend of Earl Lafitte. He wrote me before I left with his address and telephone number. He even drew me a little map of how to get to his home, but I left the letter lying on the desk in my study. I'm so embarrassed. He's told me a lot about his involvement in this cathedral so I thought I'd start with you. Can you help me?"

"Oh, Father. Mister Lafitte is one of our most active members. Currently, he's the Chair of our Chapter Board. In fact, I was just about to call a messenger service to take some papers over for him to sign."

"I'd be happy to take them over. I'll bring them back after we've connected and made dinner plans."

"Oh, there's no hurry. I really don't need them back until tomorrow, but he'll know that. Mister Lafitte can just messenger them back to me. You don't have to bring them."

Steele held out his hand. "Is that the envelope?"

She handed him the envelope. "His address is on it. You see, he doesn't live but a couple of blocks away. He has the penthouse in this high rise. She pointed to a block on a little map attached to the envelope."

"Thanks. I'll just go on over there right now."

"Please give him my regards, and thank him for doing this."

"No problem. I'm happy to be able to help."

A doorman opened the doublewide glass doors for Steele to enter the building. He entered an immaculate lobby with shiny marble floors and polished wood paneling. There was a heavy circular desk placed at its center. A thick oriental carpet framed the table. Sitting on top of the desk was one of the largest arrangements of living flowers Steele had ever seen in his life. Then he noticed similar arrangements sitting on tables beneath large mirrors on either side of the lobby. The fragrance from the flowers filled the room. A man in a brown uniform was standing behind the desk. "May I help you, Father?"

"Yes, I'm from Grace Cathedral. I have some papers here for Mister Lafitte to sign."

"One minute. I need to call up and let him know you are here."

When he hung up the telephone he said, "This way, Father." He led Steele over to an elevator with a shiny brass door. He put a key in the switch and the door opened. He gestured for Steele to enter. After Steele was inside the man turned the key and the door shut. Steele felt the elevator move very rapidly upward. When the door opened, he came face to face with an attractive young Asian man wearing a white coat, black bow tie and black pants. "You from the cathedral?"

Steele nodded.

"I tell Mister Lafitte you here."

Steele followed the man with his eyes. He walked through a large living area that was immaculately furnished. There were floor to ceiling windows on the far side of the room revealing a breathtaking view of the city and the bay. The Asian man approached a large wingback chair sitting in front of one of the windows. The chair had a single occupant. Steele could only see the back of a man's head. He had coal black hair pulled back into a long ponytail. The butler leaned over and spoke to the man. The man then turned to look back at Steele. At that moment Steele could see the man's profile against the glare of the window. He strained to make him out more clearly. And then in an instant...his eyes were opened...

ABOUT THE AUTHOR

THE REVEREND DOCTOR Dennis R. Maynard is the author of eleven books. Well over 120,000 Episcopalians have read his book, *Those Episkopols*. 3000 congregations around the United States use *Those Episkopols* in their new member ministries. Several denominational leaders have called it the unofficial handbook for the Episcopal Church. He is also the author of *Forgive and Get Your Life Back*. That particular book has been used by the same number of clergy to do forgiveness training in their congregations. Maynard has written a series of novels focusing on life in the typical congregation. These novels have received popular acceptance from both clergy and lay people.

Over his thirty-eight years of parish ministry he has served some of the largest congregations in the Episcopal Church. His ministry included parishes in Illinois, Oklahoma, South Carolina, Texas, and California. President George H.W. Bush and his family are members of the congregation he served in Houston, Texas, also the largest parish in the Episcopal Church.

He has served other notable leaders that represent the diversity of his ministry. These national leaders include Former Secretary of State, James Baker; Former Secretary of Education, Richard Riley; Supreme Court Nominee, Clement Haynsworth; and the infamous baby doctor, Benjamin Spock, among others.

Doctor Maynard maintains an extensive speaking and travel schedule. He is frequently called on to speak, lead retreats, or serve as a consultant to parishes, schools and organizations throughout the United States.

His most recent endeavors are earning him a reputation as a novelist. The books in *The Magnolia Series* are growing in popularity around the nation as readers anxiously await each new chapter.

"The novels give us a chance to look at the underside of parish life. While the story lines are fictional, the readers invariably think they recognize the characters. If not, they know someone just like the folks that attend First Episcopal Church in the town of Falls City, Georgia."

His most recent book, *When Sheep Attack,* is based on twenty-five case studies of clergy that were attacked by a small group of antagonists in their congregations. The antagonists successfully removed their senior pastor, leaving the congregations themselves divided and crippled. The book describes how it happened, what could have been done to stop it, and what can be done to prevent it from happening to your pastor and parish.

Over his thirty-eight years of parish ministry Doctor Maynard served on various diocesan boards and committees. These included various diocesan program committees, director of summer camps for boys, diocesan trustee, finance committees, and executive committees. He was elected Dean of the diocesan deanery on several occasions. He was on the Cursillo secretariat and was spiritual director for the Cursillo Movement multiple times. Maynard served as co-chair for two diocesan capital campaigns.

In the National Episcopal Church he served multiple terms on the board of the National Association of Episcopal Schools and as a trustee for Seabury Western Theological Seminary. He was named an adjunct professor in congregational development at Seabury. Maynard was the co-coordinator for two national conferences for large congregations with multiple staff ministries.

Doctor Maynard was twice named to "Oxford's Who's Who The Elite Registry of Extraordinary Professionals" and to "Who's Who Among Outstanding Americans."

Maynard earned an Associate of Arts Degree in psychology, a Bachelor of Arts Degree in the social sciences, a Masters Degree in theology, and a Doctor of Ministry Degree. He currently resides in Rancho Mirage, California.

WWW.EPISKOPOLS.COM

BOOKS FOR CLERGY AND THE PEOPLE THEY SERVE

Made in the USA
Charleston, SC
27 March 2011